PLAYING FOR YOU

HOT ON ICE, BOOK 1

AURORA PAIGE

Smitten Ink Books

Published by
Smitten Ink Books, LLC

www.aurorapaige.com

Cover Design: Steamy Designs
Photographer: Michelle Lancaster
Model: Anthony Patamisi
Editing: My Brother's Editor

To all my family and friends who waited for years for this book to be done. Thank you for your patience and everlasting support!

PLAYING WITH YOU (HOT ON ICE, BOOK 1)

BLURB

She's a curvaceous vixen who owns the hottest lounge in Los Angeles.

He's a sexy hockey goaltender who plays the game off the ice more than on.

What happens when a one-night stand becomes more?

Twenty-eight-year-old, voluptuous, Filipina-American, Arianna Santos has the hottest spot in LA nightlife. When her grandfather has a major stroke and there's a low chance of recovery, she inherits from him the worst team in the National Hockey League, the San Francisco Storm. Without knowing anything about hockey or running a hockey franchise, Arianna needs to prove to the all-boys club that a well-educated, minority female owner has a place in the industry. The Storm General Manager insists that she learn about hockey from the new goalie, Blake Collins.

Tall, toned, and hazel-eyed, Blake Collins has the swift moves on the ice as the California Crusaders goaltender, continuing the Collins goalie legacy of Stanley Cup Championships his father and grandfather established for the team. When a knee injury affects his game and attitude on the ice, he gets transferred to the San Francisco Storm as their only hope of making it to play-offs. As the player with the most knowledge and skills passed from generations of great hockey players, Blake is forced to teach the new knows-nothing-about-hockey owner, Arianna Santos, about how the hockey world works.

Blake and Arianna's animal attraction to each other gives them a passionate one-night stand in LA that doesn't end as they expected. Will their reunion cause a riff in the organization? Will they both play nice to one another for the sake of the team?

PROLOGUE

San Francisco, CA – Twelve Years Ago

Wearing the locket Mama gave me, I celebrated my sweet sixteenth birthday with just family, including my mom. Mama was still thriving and fighting with that same spirit I have come to know and admire. You could tell she was definitely weaker than the week prior. She slept most of the time, using oxygen around the clock, and was unable to speak anymore. My grandparents, Lolo Tony and Lola Lynn, aunt and uncle, Tita Rosa and Tito Kyle, their children, Jessa and Christian, and my older half-brother, Kuya Eric, all came to celebrate what was supposed to be my special day and to spend the last days of Mama's life with her. I didn't want any of the focus to be on me. I wanted my family to make Mama the center of attention.

We sat around Mama, prayed the rosary, ate delicious home-cooked Filipino food made by Lola Lynn, and enjoyed telling our favorite memories we had of Mama. It was comforting to know that they all loved Mama as much as Daddy and I did. I had the courage to sing Mama's favorite song in front of everyone. I wanted to sing it for her. Even if she wasn't fully awake to see me sing, I knew she was listening. Mama had always enjoyed hearing me sing and always expressed to me 'Anak, your voice is the most powerful tool you have. Remember to use it to make things right.'

THREE DAYS after my sixteenth birthday, Mama passed away quietly in her sleep.

1

ARIANNA

LOS ANGELES, CA: PRESENT DAY

R*ing. Buzz. Ring. Buzz. Ring. Buzz.*
Stretching my arm to the side of my bed where my nightstand was, I felt around the top, hoping to find where that annoying rattling sound was coming from. *Ugh.* My head pounded and my stomach was in knots. I felt like I was about to vomit.

Ring. Buzz. Ring. Buzz. Ring. Buzz.

"What fucking time is it? Where are my glasses?" I grumbled. Heaviness weighed on my lids as I tried to open up my eyes. Knocking stuff off my nightstand, I finally felt something metal and cool to the touch. *My eyeglasses.* I put them on, but my eyes were blurry as they were adjusting to the dim room. *Oh shit! My contacts were still in my eyes! I never took them out last night.*

I removed my glasses and searched for my eye drops in the nightstand drawer. My eyes were dry, making my contacts stick to my lids. Rummaging through the organized drawer, I felt the tiny bottle, pulled it out, and put a couple drops in each eye, blinking to lubricate my lenses.

After I wiped the wetness off my cheeks with the back of my hand, I noticed my cell phone slowly moving across my nightstand as it rang and vibrated with the incoming call. I grabbed the phone before it reached the edge.

Britney Johnstone. My assistant's name flashed on the home screen and I pressed the green circle to answer the call.

"Hey, Britney. What's going on?" I sounded like a teenage boy hitting puberty with the cracking sound in my voice. My head continued to feel as though someone was using my brain as a punching bag as I was trying to fully wake up. *How much did I drink last night?*

"Miss Santos. Did I wake you? I called you several times." Britney's voice was soft and calm. She was one of the best assistants I have ever had. She kept me organized and sane. She was definitely my right-hand woman and ebbed and flowed with my hectic schedule with ease. The last assistant, three years before Britney started, had me sprouting gray hairs at twenty-five years old.

"Oh, sorry. I was sleeping. What time is it?" It was still fairly dark in my room. The curtains were pulled shut and I couldn't tell what time of the day it was. I didn't bother checking the time when I answered Britney's call.

"It's one p.m. We were scheduled to meet to go over the celebrity VIP event for the club t—"

"One in the afternoon?! Shit! I overslept!" A rush of adrenaline surged through my body as I got out of bed quickly.

"You know this is the biggest event your club has ever hosted. I wanted to go over the details with you to make sure I don't miss anything. I'm setting up the club later and don't want to let you down. Miss Santos, I know you worked hard to prepare for this. Would it be okay to go over things now?"

"I can't believe that I overslept again. What the fuck was I thinking partying with the crowd last night?!" I let out a long breath of exhaustion.

"Look, Miss Santos. You needed to drink last night. You've been stressed from planning all these events. This one may have finally broken you. Am I right?" What Britney didn't know was that it was Mama's death anniversary yesterday. I needed to cope.

"Britney, you know me so well. These last few months have been mad crazy. Thanks for sticking by me. I don't know what I would do without you! I think the hair of the dog may be needed to get through today *and* tonight. I'll get ready and meet you at the club in about an hour and a half."

"You got it, boss. I'll see you soon with a drink in hand, ready for you."

———

STEAM FILLED my bathroom as I stepped out from a long, hot shower. I wrapped my long dark locks above my head with my towel then enveloped my body with my plush robe. *So cozy.* I wiped the steam off the mirror and looked at the tired face staring back at me. "Why did I get so wasted last night on a Wednesday?" I let out a long sigh. "You can't let it happen again, Arianna. Tonight is important... it is *very* important," I said out loud.

Enough self-pep talk. I needed to finish getting ready. A familiar ringtone tune echoed in my walk-in closet while I finalized my outfit for today: a black fitted sleeveless dress, black leather jacket, and heels. This outfit screamed *Boss Bitch*. I looked down at my phone and saw that my grandfather was calling. I smiled.

"Hi Lolo Tony. How are you?"

"Hello Arianna. Kumusta na? How is life? I haven't heard from you in a couple weeks." His voice was deep and gruff. Hearing his voice was soothing. It felt like home. I usually called my dad and grandparents to check in on them at least once a week ever since I moved out of San Francisco, but I totally forgot to call them this week.

"I'm doing great, Lolo. Work's kept me busy. We have a big event tonight and I'm getting ready to go to the lounge to start preparing for it."

"Did you get the messages we left you on your birthday a few days ago? We were worried when you didn't call us, but we hoped you enjoyed your birthday."

I knew that it was my mother's death anniversary. It had been a tough few weeks as we planned all the events happening at the lounge. Yesterday, I felt the lowest I had been in a while.

"I had a great birthday, Lolo. I appreciate all the wishes from you and Lola Lynn. Hope you all are doing well." I put some fake pep in my voice and hoped he couldn't tell on his end how I really felt.

"I have a surprise for you. We wanted to give it to you on your birthday, but didn't hear from you—"

"Lolo! You didn't have to get me anything. I don't need anything," I told him as I cut him off mid-sentence.

"Arianna, we love you very much. We wanted to do this. We felt that it was a good investment."

And there it was. It had to do with business and work. Of course, it wasn't really about *me* and what I liked. I rolled my eyes. I really didn't have time for this now. "Lolo Tony, how about if I call you back tomorrow to talk about it. I need to leave as soon as Glenn arrives and get my event ready for tonight."

"Of course, anak. We'll talk tomorrow. Give my regards to Glenn. Good luck."

"Bye Lolo. Take care. Love you."

"Hey, babe. Are you still coming over to help me with the event?"

"I'm on my way there right now," Glenn said with an annoyed tone.

"Well, if you don't want to help me, you don't have to. I have Britney waiting for me." Irritated and frustrated with my on-again and off-again high school sweetheart.

"I said, I'm on my way." Then he hung up.

Ugh! I rolled my eyes. This was typical of us. We got into arguments constantly, more so lately. I could blame it on not seeing each other for the last two weeks, but that would be too easy. This was *normal* for us. I'd been busy with the lounge and he was busy with his new job for some hockey team. Glenn was obsessed with hockey. He was born and raised in Canada before moving to the Bay Area, and Canada was the birthplace of the sport. I didn't really understand hockey and if he tried to explain what he did for work, I was sure it would go in one ear and out the other. Glenn didn't even tell me that he got the new job. I found out through social media.

Maybe Mama was right.

Before Mama passed away, Glenn and I were "talking" and not officially a couple. She told me, 'Ari, be careful with Glenn. I don't think he's good for you. I know you like him a lot, but I think you're blinded by him and how he really is.' I wanted to prove to my mom that Glenn was truly a good person, but now, she would never get to see that. There had been many times Glenn and I had broken up because he "was tired of me." It tended to be always my fault and Glenn made me feel like I wasn't good enough for him, but he forgave me and took me back. I wanted to be with him. I gave him his space and did my best to make him happy. He was my first everything. My first boyfriend. My first love. He was the first one I slept with and gave my virginity to. *Because I loved him so much.*

Facing the front door from my living room, the sound of metal grinding above the doorknob startled me as the lock on the door turned. Glenn opened the door and I stared at him.

7

We've been together for almost twelve years if you counted the multiple times we broke up then got back together. I had given him a key to my place because we decided not to move in together. He told me that we should enjoy our independence as much as we could now since we would probably get married in the future. *Whenever that will be.*

"What's that look for?" He closed the door.

Surprised that he didn't even say 'hello' or greet me in another way. "What look? I was just checking to see who was at the door."

"Who else would it be? Anyone else I should know about that has a key to your place?" Glenn's eyebrows furrowed. His dark brown eyes seared into mine.

"Of course not!" I yelled from across the room.

"I know you're bringing other guys home to fuck."

I stood up and met him at the doorway. "What the fuck, Glenn?! Why would you say that?! I'm not bringing anyone else home. You're the *only* one that has a key to my place, the *only* guy that comes over here, and the *only* guy I sleep with. What's your fucking problem?!" Tears welled up in my eyes. My face heated up.

"I don't need this. We're done," he said in a flat tone, no emotion in his voice.

"Oh, we're doing *this* today out of all the days."

"I'm serious this time, Ari. It's over." He handed the house key to me. "Don't call me."

I don't understand. "You're really going to throw away twelve years of our relationship?! Explain to me why!" I couldn't hold the tears any longer. Tears blurred my vision and quickly ran down my cheeks. "Why, dammit?!"

"I met someone else."

"What the fuck?! What do you mean you met someone else?"

"You heard me. I met someone else. We're done."

"You're really going to leave me for a woman you just met?"

"I've known her for years. We've been—"

"You bastard! You've been fucking her on the side for years while we've been together?"

Glenn's eyes shifted elsewhere. He didn't say anything.

"Wow. I guess that's my answer. Get the fuck out!" Tears streamed down my face. My words escalating in volume. "Get out!" Opening the door for him to exit.

"You were always too busy for me with your family, friends, work—" he said as he walked out the front door.

"Don't spin this on me and validate your reasoning for cheating on me. Now get out."

I slammed the door and turned the latch to lock it. Sitting down on the floor with my back pressed against the door, I sobbed. *Was I really that stupid to not see this?* I guess I was.

LA TRAFFIC WAS HORRENDOUS. No matter what time of day it was, there were always lots of cars clogging up the roads. I tended to do conference calls in my car on the way to my restaurant and nightclub, *Blue Velvet Lounge.* It was the only way that I wouldn't be alone with my thoughts. Doing that will destroy me.

My eyes were puffy from all the crying. I applied concealer before I left my house and had my dark black Chanel sunglasses on, hoping that it would hide the remnants of a bad morning.

I arrived at Blue Velvet Lounge as the lunch crowd was dying down. Pulling up to the valet area, the two attendants straightened their posture as soon as my silver Mercedes S-Class Coupe slowed down in front of them. I enjoyed seeing how my presence affected the behavior of my employees. I worked hard for my business and I'm happy to have found loyal staff that respected me.

"Good afternoon, Miss Santos," said one of the valet attendants as he opened my car door. Both young men smiled at me, and I admired the polished look of their uniforms.

"Good afternoon, guys. How's it going today?"

One of the attendants, who had the face and physique of a model, said with a slight Southern twang in his voice, "It's been pretty steady today, Miss Santos."

"Good! Keep up the great job, guys!"

"Thank you, ma'am," both said in unison, then laughed.

"Please don't call me 'ma'am.' It makes me sound old," I called out jokingly and laughed as I passed by them.

As I entered through the front door, I carefully stepped on the floor with my Louboutins. These shoes had a slick bottom and I've been known to slip if I walked too hastily. I wasn't going to make this moment the day my employees see me fall on the floor. As amusing as that may be, I couldn't afford to get hurt. There was too much to do. I was greeted by the hostess, wait staff, chefs, and bar staff as I made my rounds.

Blue Velvet Lounge was my pride and joy. I started developing my business plan when I was doing my undergrad and carried out the plans, with the help of my daddy and Lolo Tony, when I was finishing up my MBA. There were generations of successful businesses that my family had developed both in the Philippines and in the US. Running a business was in my blood and I was determined to make my business successful.

The restaurant and lounge had a seductive, trendy, and romantic vibe with lush blue velvet-covered dining and lounge chairs, crisp white linens, low lighting, candles, a romantic patio, an avant-garde private dining area, and fresh-cut flowers embellished the large venue space. As I reached the private dining room to meet Britney, I couldn't help but admire the view of what I have accomplished already. *I wish Mama was here to see this.*

Opening the door to the private room, a beautiful blonde was sitting with all her documents laid out on the table in front of her. She glanced up and smiled. As I walked up closer to my assistant, she got up from her seat and we greeted each other with a kiss on the cheek and a hug.

"Hey, Britney, hope you didn't wait too long for me."

"Not at all, Miss Santos. I got here about ten minutes ago. I asked Brett to bring you a glass of your favorite, Gamay Rouge. By the way, I love your outfit. You look so good!"

"Thanks, doll! All black is a curvy girl's best friend." I laughed. I felt good. Although I was always critiqued about my weight by my mom and relatives, I didn't care about my curves and size as much as I did when I was younger. Who cared if my thighs were thick and grazed each other as I walked. "How's everything going?"

"I'm so nervous and excited about tonight's event. This is *huge* for Blue Velvet. Did you see our guest list?!" Britney asked.

"I know, Brit. I'm excited too. We definitely need to make this event memorable, especially for our celebs. Now let's get down to business."

2

BLAKE

LOS ANGELES, CA - TWO YEARS AGO

"The starting goalie for your California Crusaders is Blake Collins." Hearing the crowd cheer when the arena announcer said your name never got old. It got me hyped and pumped up for the game. My teammates and I pulled that crazy energy from the crowd and transferred it to the way we played the game.

"Tonight's game is against the visiting team, the Seattle Renegades," said the announcer. A mixture of boos and cheers were heard among the crowd. The Renegades were one of our rivals on the west coast. Our number one rival was the San Francisco Storm, but they were not really competition to us this season. They were at the bottom of the Pacific Division, having only won ten games out of a few dozen. But who's counting? *I just wanted my Stanley Cup ring.*

After the National Anthem, it was time to shine. *Let's show these fans what hockey is really about.* I squeezed the drink from my water bottle into my mouth. The cage on my helmet prevented some of the water from actually reaching my lips. Drops of water dribbled down my chin. I didn't bother to lift the cage off my face. I wanted to be ready for action, and I sure was. The players on the ice got into position. I got into my stance, and the referee dropped the puck.

WE REACHED twenty minutes through the end of the first period with no score by either team. I had multiple saves during the first and will keep it that way going into the second and third periods. The Crusaders had fourteen shots on goal, but the Renegade's goalie seemed to be having a good night so far since no one from my team could get the damn puck into their net. I'm sure Coach Wilson will give us his "pep talk" while the team recharged for the second period. I didn't have time for that. We headed into the locker room as soon as the horn blared. *Intermission.* I sped down the hallway as fast as I could walk. Having all this damn padding on was a nuisance, especially when you needed to pee. But I really needed that Red Bull before the game to wake me up.

Staying up late with my flavor of the week was worth it. *What was her name again? Leslie? Elizabeth?* Whatever. It was a great night. I met her at a bar. Her tits were huge and probably fake. I was more of an ass kind of guy, but she was cute. The perks of living in Los Angeles and being a sports celebrity was that the women who wanted to meet you, wanted to sleep with you.

Fuck me! I really needed to take a piss.

"Move out of the way!" I yelled as I tried to go around some of my teammates.

"Guys! Let Blakester through!" one of the defensemen said as he slowed down and moved right in front of me. He laughed.

"What the fuck, bro?!"

"Dude, just kidding, Blake. Relax, you're almost to the locker room, bro." The big guy stepped aside for me to pass.

He was right. We were practically there. With the fullness in my bladder, I couldn't think and could not hold it in any longer. Anyone trying to make me laugh would definitely make me piss on myself. I avoided all eye contact and any conversations others were having as I rushed to the back where the urinals were. I threw my stick, blocker, and catcher to the floor toward my locker as I passed it.

After ten minutes of untying, unbuckling, and undressing the top half of my body, I was able to push my pants and jockstrap down. My body relaxed as I emptied my bladder. *Ahh*. I've heard that a few of the greatest hockey goalies pissed on themselves during a game because they couldn't hold it in until intermission, but I wasn't going to be *that* guy.

I pulled my pants and jockstrap up before heading to the sink to wash my hands. Needing a pick-me-up before the second period, I splashed some cold water on my face and it brought me back to life. I was *not* going to drink coffee or an energy drink like I did before the game. I needed to focus on winning this match, not on trying to avoid pissing on myself. The mood was light as I returned to the locker room, filled with chatter and laughter as the team got ready for the next period.

Grabbing a fresh stick and tape out of my locker, I started to tape a knob on top of the handle. This kept me focused and my mind on winning this game. I needed a new stick before each period. People may think that was superstitious, but that was *my* routine.

"Collins! Let's give them a shutout!" Coach Wilson yelled as he approached me and patted my shoulder.

"You got it, Coach." My voice confident. I smiled as I took the white sticky tape and started at the toe of the blade. I concentrated on wrapping the tape firmly, making sure no bubbles formed. I overlapped the tape as I moved it closer to the heel of the blade, then cut it off. I waxed the sides of the blade, then grabbed my chest protector and geared back up. Second period was about to start in less than five minutes.

I finished getting ready and got back onto the ice before the second period started, giving me enough time to do a quick warm-up and stretch. Stretching my hips, groin, and legs out looking like I'm Spiderman or part of Cirque du Soleil. The referees made it known that it was time to start the second period. Players got back into their places.

Puck drop.

Ksssh-Ksssh-Ksssh. The sounds of players swiftly moving on the ice and hitting the puck around were getting louder as they crossed the blue line of the home team. My eyes shifted quickly, following the movement of the puck. *Thud-Thud-Thud* echoed in the arena as players got rammed into the boards. *Where is the puck?* My eyes focused on one of the Renegade players who moved closer to my zone. Anticipating my opponent's moves, I got into my stance and swayed in the same direction he was moving.

Crash.

3

BLAKE

LOS ANGELES, CA - PRESENT DAY

"**A**lright Blake, let's try doing a drill this time."

I walked to the middle of the training area, kept my face stoic, after doing my warm-up and stretches.

"If you're in pain, we can take a break."

"Nah, I'm good, Dale. Let's do this. I took a pain reliever before I got here." *My knee was fucking hurting and throbbing, but I won't give in to the pain. I needed to push through.*

"Well, if you're good, then let's go. Let's start with press-ups. Start with kneeling on the mat, and when you throw the medicine ball to the wall, let your body go down to the floor. Then push back up using your arms to catch the ball as it bounces back to you." The physical therapist demonstrated it for me. "You got it?"

"Yup." I grabbed a blue mat and a ten-pound medicine ball then knelt on the squishy foam pad as instructed. I went to work, focused on the season and what was expected of me by my fans, my team, and my father. The air knocked out of me as my body pressed onto the floor, and I grunted, pushing myself back up quickly to get the ball as it came bouncing back toward me. I repeated this move ten times, then did the set again two more times.

The hour of therapy went by quickly as I ran drills that made me look like I wanted to be Spiderman, a speed skater, and a bird. Hopping on one leg from side to side, throwing balls against the wall, and testing my hand-eye coordination were added to the mix of this therapy session.

As I finished my set of the last drill, I sat down on the ground, sweat dripped down my face and my shirt soaked it up around my neckline and back. Dale reached his hand out to me. Both of us grabbed hold of each other's forearms, and he helped me up from the ground. Dale threw a towel at me.

"Great work today, Blake."

Wiping my face with the small white towel, I nodded in agreement that it was indeed a great session today. "Thanks, Dale. I think I'll be ready for tomorrow's game. I'll see you next time."

"Sounds good. Good luck!" Dale gave me a fist bump and left to get set up for his next client.

Walking back to my car in the lot, my phone rang. Looking down at the screen, I saw that it was Dad. *Great.*

"Hey, Dad. How's it going?"

"Blake, checking on you and how your physical therapy was going. I know you have a game against the San Francisco Storm tomorrow, but they're at the bottom of the league again. So I'm not worried. It'll be like a practice game." Dad chuckled.

"You know that the Storm are underdogs. But you never know. They may come back with a winning streak and surprise us all."

"Don't let them win." The tone in his voice changed. Deeper and darker. Silence grew on the line, making me uncomfortable and unsure what to say next. I knew I didn't want to make him upset. God knows what would happen. When it came to hockey, it was all business to him. In his eyes, I disappointed him in this sport. I wasn't good enough... I was never good enough.

"Don't worry, Dad. I'm ready." I made it to my black Audi SQ8 and got inside. I just sat there waiting for this conversation to end.

"You better be. That knee injury cost you a season with the Crusaders. You need to get back in as a starting position. Being on the bench doesn't help you get better as a goaltender. Remember that."

"Yes, sir."

"Alright, well, your mother's calling for me to help her with something. I'll be watching the game tomorrow."

"Alright, Dad. Please tell Mom I said 'hello.' I won't let you down."

"I know you won't, son. Talk to you soon."

The phone clicked on the other end before I was about to say goodbye.

"Bye to you too, Dad." I took a deep breath in and let out a long sigh. Then

started my car and drove home. I didn't want to worry about disappointing Dad now. I needed to deal with him tomorrow after the game.

THE NEXT DAY, my teammates and I performed our game day rituals and routines, hoping that these quirks we had were good luck and helped us win the game. My game day schedule never changed: morning skate for an hour, mealtime, and a nap when I got home, get showered and dressed in my dark, fitted suit. It's like clockwork. I triple-checked that I had all my gear in the car before I left for the arena.

Looking down at my outfit, I checked the time on my watch and noticed something missing from my hand. *My grandfather's*

Stanley Cup ring. I ran upstairs, grabbed it from the top of my dresser, and slid it on my ring finger. Pop gave it to me before he passed away five years ago. Whenever I looked at this ring, it became my constant reminder and motivation to continue to work hard so the Crusaders can win the Stanley Cup. Then I would be the third generation of goaltenders on the Crusaders to get a ring. 'The Collins Legacy' as my dad called us.

I ran back downstairs and headed out, not wanting to get caught up in LA traffic. It was close to three p.m. on a Thursday. Rush hour had started, and I'm sure it was already bumper to bumper trying to get near the LA Ice Center.

After sitting in an hour of traffic, I pulled up to the gate of the player and staff entrance of the arena.

"Good luck today, Blake," the security guard stated as he let me through the gate.

I nodded my head. "Thanks, man."

This was my first day back as a starting goaltender. Twenty games into the season and Coach finally felt I was ready to start. *And I was.* I've played a couple games as a backup but Coach has always pulled me out of the game for some penalties I've made. *Those guys deserved it.*

I was always early to the arena and usually the first one in the locker room. Dropping my bag and hockey sticks in front of my locker, I started my pregame routine. Undressing out of my tailored suit, I pulled on my long-sleeved shirt. Before getting into my hockey pants, I taped around my knee with neon-colored elastic sports tape strips as I needed more support and pain relief. I then grabbed my hockey stick and did the routine taping of the knob and the blade. The meticulous wrapping around the twig was therapeutic, almost Zen-like.

I stretched, worked on hand-eye coordination exercises, and ran some laps through the arena hallways. I put my AirPods in my ears and turned on my pregame playlist on my phone. I sprinted through the hallway, following the beat of the song.

Turning one of the corners, I got distracted by an incoming call coming from my phone and ran into one of our visiting team's players. I never saw this guy before. *He must be a rookie.* He was a tall, husky guy. *Must be a defenseman.*

"Hey, watch it!" the guy with dark brown hair and beard yelled out.

"Sorry, man. You good?" I stopped to check on how he was doing.

"You better be sorry."

"Yo, it was an accident. What's your problem?"

"You're my problem. You better watch your back on the ice. You won't know what hit you."

What the fuck was this guy's deal? Why am I a problem to him? I ran back to the Crusader's locker room. My teammates started to trickle into the locker room. The guys knew not to talk to me when I prepared myself for a game. I was in a zone and mentally planning for what lay ahead. That run-in with the San Francisco Storm player had already thrown me off my game.

THE FACE-OFF BEGAN as the referee dropped the puck. *Tap-tap-tap.* Hockey sticks clashed as players tried to get a handle on the puck. *Kssh-kssh-kssh.* The sounds of blades gliding on the ice got louder as Crusaders and Storm players migrated closing the gap between me and them. The puck got closer to my zone and I anticipated the opponent's play. The player whacked the puck toward my net. Lifting up my left arm, I felt the force of the rubber puck digging into my glove. Then I pulled my glove toward my chest. The referee blew the whistle. Clapping and cheering echoed in the arena. That happened a few more times during the first period. I was not letting any puck into my net tonight.

"Two minutes left of the period." The deep, baritone voice of the announcer was heard through the speakers of the large venue.

My eyes were focused on the puck. I clenched my jaw as soon as I saw the San Francisco Storm player coming toward me. I got down into my stance and skated side-to-side following the rhythm of my opponent, #44 Patrick Greene. He stopped and took a slap shot to the puck. It hit my helmet. I gritted my teeth as heat rushed to my face. I took off my glove and threw it onto the ice along with my stick, and skated quickly to him. With a closer look at the guy, I recognized that it was the same player that I had an altercation with earlier in the hallway.

"What the fuck, man?! What was that?" I yelled, standing face-to-face with him.

The opponent had a sly smirk on his face.

This was definitely intentional. He threatened me in the hallway pregame and told me to 'watch my back.' I glared at him for a moment, then I turned and skated away to be "the bigger person." *Well, fuck it.* Instantaneously, I turned around, skated forward as fast as I could then I slammed into #44, knocking us both down onto the ice. I threw some jabs to his face. The opponent's helmet came off. The referees stood around, watching me punch the shit out of Greene, and waiting for the perfect time to separate us. The crowd went nuts, cheering and pounding on the glass.

Blood dripped out of my opponent's nose. Two referees pulled me up and away from Greene. Some of my teammates stood between me and that asshole who hit me in the head with the puck. I was escorted back to my zone by stripes. Taking my water bottle from the top of my net, I squeezed the bottle, squirting water on my face. One of the referees called a major on my actions for misconduct. There were twenty-eight seconds left of the first period and Coach Wilson sent one of the defensemen, Rafael Dillon, to take my place in the penalty box. Five minutes set for the penalty, and a power play began.

Brrrrrrrrhhhhh. Time's up. The vibration of the loud horn felt beneath my skates. A scoreless first period was over. Both clubs headed back to their designated locker rooms.

"Collins!" Was the first thing that came out of Coach Wilson's mouth as the Crusaders entered the large room. "I need to talk to you." Standing off to the side away from the other players, Coach waited for me as I approached him.

I tried to read Coach's face as I stood face-to-face with him. He had a flat expression and it was very hard to figure out what his mood was going to be.

"Was that really necessary?! You know we got enforcers to do that kind of work!" His face turned bright red. Brows furrowed.

"Coach, I did what I had to do. That asshole hit me in the head with the puck intentionally. I'm not going to let him get the satisfaction of that." With a deep tone and raspiness to my voice, I stepped closer to Coach Wilson and met him eye-to-eye. The rage still burned inside, I glared into his eyes as if I was trying to burn a hole in him.

Resting his hand on my shoulder, he stepped back a bit. His demeanor softened up. "Look, Collins, you just got back as a starting position. I need you to be on your A game and get back to shutting out our games. Get focused. You got it?"

"Yeah, I got it."

"Keep your head in the game and don't let them break you. I've seen the way you've been playing lately. You need to snap out of whatever's been troubling you."

"I said I got it, Coach. I need to prepare for next period." I walked away before even getting a response from him. As soon as I got to my locker, I started prepping for the period ahead.

IN THE SECOND PERIOD, the Crusaders scored two goals, one of which occurred during the first five minutes of the period in the course of the power play. I also didn't let any pucks shot by the Storm get into my net. As requested by Coach Wilson, I focused on the game. My eyes stayed glued to the puck. I desperately wanted to win this game... losing was not an option.

After the final intermission, the third period started. The animosity I felt for Patrick Greene in the first period faded as we headed into the third. I was determined to get a shutout and that was all I cared about. We got another goal this period, making the score 3-0 Crusaders. The Storm players became more aggressive since they had no goals thus far. Ten minutes into the period, #25 Matthew Moore from the Storm traveled quickly across the ice en route to me.

I had flashbacks to the day of my knee injury. It's like déjà vu. Moore was not slowing down. Focusing on his momentum toward the goal crease was distracting me from my concentration on the puck and what my next move will be. I moved forward nearing #25 to get the puck away from him. Moore lost balance and smashed into me. A hard blow knocked into my chest and took my breath away. Falling forward, my helmet and chest hit the ice hard.

I stayed there for a minute. Trying to soak in what had happened. Coach Wilson, the referees, and my teammates showed up by my side to check on me and helped sit me up. I took my helmet off and the physician arrived on the ice to assess my condition to see if I had a concussion. I was cleared to play as I had no injuries sustained. I slowly stood up on my own and could hear cheering and clapping from the crowd.

The rage that I thought had faded away from the first period had returned. Blood boiled under my skin. A rush of heat rose up to my face. Both hands clenched into fists. I was about to pop off at this guy. I scanned the ice and found #25 standing near the face-off circle. With a sharpness in my movement toward him, I confronted Moore and shoved him hard. I had no words to say. Instead, I started throwing punches to his face. Moore was able to manage a hit to my head, but it was a weak shot and didn't affect me. While some players from the Crusaders and Storm came onto the ice to pry Moore and I apart, other brawls formed around us between the other players.

The referees blew their whistles and tried to stop the chaos on the ice. A few minutes later, players were headed back to their designated benches, waiting for the stripes to call out any penalties. Patting the flat of his hand on top of his head then placing his hands on his hips and pointing his finger at me, the referee called out, "Match penalty and misconduct on Crusaders #31." *Shit!*

I saw Coach Wilson talk to the backup goalie, #32 Timothy Meyers, then Meyers grabbed his helmet and got on the ice to warm up. I skated toward the entry to our locker room.

"Sorry, man," Meyers said as he passed by me.

"All good, man. Shut them out."

I passed by the Crusader's bench. Coach scowled and watched me exit the ice. Without a word, I went straight into the locker room and slammed the door behind me.

I SHOWERED and got ready to leave when the guys returned to the locker room after the game. They were all smiles and celebrated the win. Meyers finished the game with a shutout. *Those Storm assholes deserved it!*

"Let's celly, Blakester! You had an awesome game, fights and all," one of the guys yelled out.

"Great comeback as a starter, man."

"Thanks, bro." I gave a fist bump.

Coach Wilson was the last person to enter the locker room.

His face was indifferent. He looked at me with intent but didn't say a word. I disappointed him. I disappointed myself. I definitely disappointed my father who mentioned that he was going to watch tonight's game.

The press came and interviewed us all. They asked about the progress on my knee injury, my return as a starter, and of course, the fighting. I provided them with general responses: 'My knee is healing, and it got me back to playing as a starter,' and 'The actions I took were in the heat of the moment. I deserved the consequences.' Then the press left.

"Hey Blakester, one of my boys is throwing a party downtown. Go with us." The Crusader's captain, Justin Roberts, placed his arm around my shoulders.

"Nah, it's cool." Hesitating at first. I just wanted to go home.

"Dude, come on, drinking and ladies! What's more important that you would pass on this? Plus, we don't have morning skate tomorrow."

That's true. With all that happened during the game and all this pent-up rage I had inside, I thought going out and drinking would take my mind off things. Assuming my dad was going to call me tonight, I would rather not talk shop with him right now. Also, since the accident, I haven't really slept with anyone as I was focused on healing so I can play hockey, so this would be a good opportunity to meet some women and get back into the game. "Alright. Where are we going?"

"Blue Velvet Lounge."

4

ARIANNA

"**B**ritney, everything ready? Let's take a walk around and go through the list again before the guests arrive. Red carpet and photo backdrop set-up?" Approaching the rolled out red carpet outside the venue, we saw the large backdrop hung against the entire wall, with the Blue Velvet Lounge logo and 'JB's Birthday Bash!' printed on it.

"Done. The photographers look like they're ready."

The photographers tested out their equipment and lighting when Britney and I passed by. "You guys ready?" I smiled at the photographers as they nodded their heads 'yes.' I scanned around and saw security going over their plans for tonight's event. I hired extra security since it was a high-profile event and a lot of celebrities were expected in attendance. The head of security and I made eye contact. I nodded and he did the same in return.

Going back inside the lounge, I asked Britney, "Are all the bars fully stocked and bartenders ready?"

"Yes, they are. You want a drink?" Britney said, amused.

I laughed. "Not right this minute, but as soon as the guest of honor and his guests arrive, I may sneak myself a drink."

Britney laughed.

"How about the DJ? Is he all set up? Is the projector set up?"

"He's almost ready," Britney said.

The DJ started dropping the beats. He was known for spinning at the hottest clubs in Las Vegas, and I was so excited that he agreed to do this party tonight. Walking toward our VIP area. There were four different sections roped off from one another. Each section had long blue velvet couches that surrounded a small round table. Buckets of ice, a variety of liquors, sodas, juices, water, glasses, and a 'reserved' sign sat on top of each table.

"Well, the DJ sounds great! Now what about our VIP areas? Are the waitresses ready to serve our VIPs?" I increased the volume of my voice so Britney could hear me above the music.

"Yes, boss." Britney looked around the room. "Everything is set."

"Amazing job, Brit! It's almost ten, I think it's time we open up the doors."

JB JIMENEZ, star basketball player for the Los Angeles Lakers and birthday celebrant, arrived around eleven p.m. with his entourage of beautiful women and other players from his team. I only knew JB because he contacted me to organize his party and mentioned that he played basketball. So I did what other curious people did, and searched for him on the internet and social media. With the number of people following him on social media, I knew he was famous.

Standing near the hostess area at the front of my lounge, I observed as more and more sports celebrities from the pro basketball, football, baseball, and hockey teams slowly followed suit into the lounge. I pinched myself on my arm. I couldn't believe this was happening. Although I didn't follow sports and didn't know who everyone was, I was still starstruck. I couldn't even tell you their names, let alone what sport each of the celebrities played. But what I can tell you was that these pro athletes were all taller than five-eleven and very good-looking. I couldn't help but admire all the attractive people partying at Blue Velvet Lounge.

As I stood there celebrity-watching, I had this feeling someone was watching me. From my peripheral vision, I noticed a man with dark hair. I wanted to get a clearer look of this guy. I moved my head toward his direction. Trying not to make eye contact, and pretending not to notice that he was totally staring at me, I scanned the area surrounding him as if I was searching for something. Then I turned my gaze away.

Oh. My. God. He was gorgeous. Wearing dark blue slim fit jeans and a fitted gray button-down oxford shirt, his silhouette gave away how toned and fit he was. His hair was dark brown, spiked up in a messy hairstyle. His sleeves were rolled up on his forearm, revealing tattoos starting at his wrist and moving up his arm. My mind wandered as I thought of how far those tattoos went up his arm and what other tattoos he may have hidden on his body.

Out of nowhere, Britney nudged me in the side with her elbow. "Hey, boss."

It startled me, and I lost balance for a quick second. Gaining my composure and hoping that guy did not see me stumble, I turned to my lovely assistant while fixing my outfit. "What's up, Brit? Are there any issues?"

Flipping through pages on her clipboard, Britney glanced up and smiled. "No, ma'am. Just saw you gawking at our guests and wanted to make sure no one would catch you staring at them." *Did she see me eyeing that guy? Did she notice that handsome man staring at me?* Britney had a keen eye for attention to details as well as my best interests. She had always watched my back, and she knew that I would always have hers. Britney was most certainly indispensable and my confidant. I could trust her to run my business without any hand-holding. She knew me and my work ethic.

Placing a loose strand of hair behind my ear, I smirked. "Appreciate it, doll! Did I have my mouth hanging open as I stared at the handsome men coming into the lounge?" I laughed so hard, I snorted. That made both of us laugh.

"At least you weren't drooling!" Britney said, trying to hold in her laughter. That made us both laugh out loud.

"Well, I'm going to make my rounds to make sure everything is fine and that everyone is having a good time."

"Okay, Miss Santos. I'll hang around here and let you know if there are any issues."

I turned around, expecting the guy that was easy on the eyes to be standing there, but he wasn't there any longer. *Ugh!* My heart sank a bit. Why was I upset about this? How would I know that he was looking at me to begin with? I couldn't let this mystery guy distract me from my job, but part of me hoped that I ran into him when I did my rounds. *Dammit, Arianna! You need to focus!*

I walked around the venue section by section. Checking on my staff, they reassured me that everything was under control. From what I could see, almost every guest had drinks in hand, some had two. There were people throwing back shot after shot. The DJ dropped hip hop beats in the main room as guests were dancing, grinding, and throwing their hands up with the flow of the music. I passed the VIP area and JB stopped me abruptly.

"This is the owner of the club, guys!" He stood up from the couch, yelled out loud, and pointed at me. His guests cheered out while bobbing their heads and swaying to the beat of the music with a drink in hand. "Give it up to the woman who knows how to throw a party!" His eyes glazed and words slurred.

He was drunk. "Thanks, JB! Happy birthday!" I smiled as he moved closer to me.

JB wrapped his long arm around my shoulders and looked down toward me. He was at least a foot taller than me. Leaning down, he spoke directly in my ear. "Drink with us." He smiled.

JB was very handsome and had a charm about him, I could see why women adored him. He wore a button-down shirt with the sleeves rolled up to his elbows, exposing tattoos of crosses, words, and some Asian-inspired designs on both forearms. His inked arms were toned and the one that lay across my shoulders felt strong. *Mmm. Men with tattoos.* I turned to him and shook my head 'no.' His face was close to mine. I leaned closer to his ear. "I'm good. I'm working right now, and I shouldn't be partying with my clients."

"I see. Well, you're the boss. If you change your mind, you know where to find me." Turning to me, he removed his arm, gave me a wink, and went back to his group.

Note to self: Watch out for drunk JB. He may be cute, but he's not my type. Needing to get out of the VIP area quickly, I turned around and briskly walked out of that area. Turning the corner, I collided with *him*.

5

BLAKE

"What do you want to drink, Blakester?" Roberts yelled over the music that blared in the bar area. Staring at the variety of liquor bottles lined up on the shelves on display, I decided on my usual, "Jack and Coke." It's a safe choice that I knew wouldn't get me too messed up.

"Alright, cool. We'll take a shot first... to loosen up." Grinning, Roberts and a couple of the guys from the team slipped into a group of ladies at the bar area. From where I stood, the women smiled and giggled as Roberts and my teammates displayed their charming qualities. Knowing them, they will pick up the drink tab for the ladies. I laughed in amusement.

A few minutes later, Roberts and the guys returned with my Jack and Coke as well as a caramel-colored liquid concoction. "What's this?"

"It's the Three Wise Men shot... Jack Daniels, Jim Beam, and Johnny Walker."

Oh shit! This is how we're going to start off the night. I knew I should have just gone home after the game, but I wanted to meet some women. "Alright, then."

Clinking our glasses, our respected team captain said, "To a great game against the Storm, the starting return of Blakester, and a fun night."

All of us cheered and took the shot mixture down in a large gulp. Burning down my throat, I took a swig of my Jack and Coke as a chaser, almost finishing my drink.

"Blake, we're going to hang with those ladies for a bit." Roberts turned toward the same group of women he met a few minutes earlier at the bar. Roberts nodded to them and the women smiled. "Going to join us?"

"Yeah, I will. They're cute. But first, I got to take a piss." Looking around the dimly lit area in the lounge. "Dude, do you know where the hell the bathroom is in this place?"

"It may be over there," Roberts said, pointing in the opposite direction of the bar. A light came from the entrance, looked like it's the lobby area of the venue.

"Alright, thanks."

I finished my Jack and Coke and left the empty glass on a nearby table before making my way toward the main entryway. I squeezed through the multiple groups of people that huddled around the dance floor socializing. I couldn't help but look at all the beautiful women. They were probably groupies. Ones that only wanted the fame of being connected with sports celebrities, and ones that I had associated myself with before my accident. I smiled at the women that could be possibilities for taking home tonight, trying to remember their faces for when I came back.

My eyes adjusted to the bright light of the lobby area. I looked from side to side and noticed the sign indicating where the restrooms were located and headed in that direction. *There was a line to the bathroom.* The bathrooms were gender-neutral and single stalls. I stood against the wall looking at the time. Then I saw *her.*

This beautiful, tanned woman with long black hair. Her

smile captivated me. She was definitely attractive. Standing there and staring at this beautiful woman, she wore a black dress that hugged her body, showing off her curvy and luscious figure. She stood behind the hostess area and watched as guests came into the venue. *Maybe she worked here or maybe she was waiting for someone that was using the bathroom?* A lady with a clipboard who clearly looked like she worked at the lounge, snuck up next to her.

Oh damn, Gorgeous just lost her balance. My body tensed up and I was ready to run to save her. If I was close enough, I would try to catch her before she fell. But she was able to regain her balance pretty quickly. *Oh great, she was looking my way. Did she notice me admiring her?*

Startled by a tap on my shoulder, I loosened my gaze on the beautiful woman, and turned to my left to see who needed my attention.

"Hey man, the line's moving." A tall, brawny guy pointed past my head in the direction of the restrooms. I saw the large space between myself and the person in front of me.

"Sorry, man." I walked forward, closing the gap. I glance at *Gorgeous* again and her back was turned to me. *Damn! That ass! Kim Kardashian had nothing on this sexy woman.* A restroom stall opened up, and I took it before the guy behind me said something.

After taking care of my bladder and checking myself in the mirror, I walked back into the lobby, hoping to see that curvaceous woman again. Disappointed that she wasn't there or even in that vicinity, I wandered around inside the lounge, checking out the venue and anything that I may find interesting. I liked the vibe of this place. It had a sex appeal to it... just like that woman. *All I could think about now was that woman...her smile, her beauty, and her curves.*

Passing by the bar and dance area again, I saw waitresses bringing bottles to people inside a private area. That was probably the VIP area. Standing outside of it, I noticed a familiar silhouette standing in front of a group. *It was her... and she was not alone.* Of course, she was with someone. She's beautiful. Why wouldn't she be in a relationship? Next to her, with his arm around her shoulders was JB Jimenez. Roberts introduced me to JB when we arrived at Blue Velvet Lounge. This was *his* birthday bash.

He seemed like a cool guy, and I wasn't going to ruin his party by peeping at his woman. *He was a lucky man.*

Being a bit distraught by the sight of them together, I walked away, needing to go back to the bar area. I definitely needed and wanted a drink, or maybe, like three. I could also hang out with Captain and the ladies he rounded up to hang with the guys. I'm sure one of those cute women would be a good choice to take home tonight. I walked around and didn't recognize where I was going. As much as I didn't want to pass by to see JB and the woman I couldn't get out of my head, I turned around and approached the VIP area once more. I couldn't help but turn my head to look inside that area, yearning to see that woman again, who I didn't even know.

The dimly lit area made it difficult to find my way around. Suddenly, someone bumped into my chest and gripped my biceps as she stumbled. *Is this lady drunk?* Holding the small of her back to stabilize her balance, I glanced down, and it was *her* looking up at me. Intently staring into her dark eyes, I couldn't say a word or move. I was fixated on this woman I held in my arms. The dim light from the ceiling was right over her, giving her face a slight glow. Heat rushed to my hands, face, and my groin.

"I'm so sorry. I didn't mean to run into you." She loosened her grip and straightened her posture. Her voice was pleasant and had a rich tone to it. It didn't sound fake, like she was trying to sound sweet.

Still feeling the pressure of where she held my arms, I slowly released my hands from her lower back. Keeping my gaze on her, she was even more beautiful up close. "Are you okay? I should be the one apologizing. I think it was my fault. I wasn't paying attention."

"I guess we are both to blame." She smiled, displaying dimples on her cheeks. "I wasn't paying attention either... and I'm good." She stepped back a little, then looked away. I couldn't tell in the dim room if she was blushing, but she seemed embarrassed. It was cute. "By the way, I'm Arianna." She extended her hand for a handshake.

Grabbing her hand, her skin felt smooth and soft to the touch. "Nice to meet you. I'm Blake." Shaking her hand and smiling back at her. "Well, Arianna, can I buy you a drink to make up for almost making you fall?"

"I don't think that would be wise." She glanced at me with a worried look on her face.

Remembering moments earlier that I saw her with JB, I said, "Oh, I'm sorry. You must be here with your boyfriend."

"Oh, it's not that. I'm not in a relationship, but I'm actually working right now. It wouldn't be professional for me to drink at work."

Relief swept through my body as I learned she was not with JB after all or anyone for that matter. "What do you do?" I was curious to learn what this attractive woman did for a living.

"I own this lounge."

6

ARIANNA

L ooking at Blake's expression, I wasn't sure if he was impressed with knowing I own this lounge or if he thought I was joking. The corners of his mouth curved up into a smile.

"Wow, that's awesome. This place has a cool vibe to it."

"Is this your first time here?"

"Yeah, I don't usually go out on a... umm." Blake was having trouble finding his words. *Was he nervous talking to me?*

"A school night?" I interrupted him and giggled to lighten the mood.

"Something like that." He chuckled. "You looked like you were in a hurry. Do you need to go?"

"I was making my rounds, but I think I'm pretty much done for now. Are you having a good time at this party?"

"Now that I've met you." Blake grinned.

My cheeks warmed up. I'm sure they were turning pink. This guy was hot and charming. *Should I be worried about this one? Just something about him was different, and I wanted to know more.* Not wanting Blake to leave just yet, I asked, "Would you like a tour of Blue Velvet Lounge?"

"Yeah, that would be great, if you have time to do it of course."

"Let's get you a drink first. Don't worry, I know people." I gave him a sly smile and a wink as we started walking closer to the bar. We stopped at the side of the long, narrow table, almost standing behind it where the bartenders were.

One of my bartending staff greeted us and told me to let him know when we were ready.

Turning to Blake, I looked up at him. Although I had my high heels on, I was probably about five inches shorter than he was right now. He had to be at least six feet tall. "What's your usual drink?"

"I'll get something only if you get to have a drink with me." Blake's eyes glimmered from the DJ's lights that flashed around the room.

"I told you I ca—" Blake placed his index finger close to my lips stopping me mid-sentence, which surprised me.

He leaned in toward the bartender and got his attention. Pointing at me, he said, "Let me ask you about her. Has your boss ever had a drink while she was working?"

The bartender nodded 'yes' and looked at me with apologetic eyes.

"Well then." Blake turned to me and raised an eyebrow. He leaned closer and whispered in my ear. His voice raspy and low. "Have a drink with me. If you're going to give me a tour of this place, I won't be the only one drinking." His breath tickled my ear as he spoke and sent chills down my neck. Being so close to Blake, I got a whiff of his cologne, a delicious masculine scent. It was so tantalizing that I could almost taste it.

"Sure. I guess I'll make an exception." I sighed. I really didn't want to drink during this event since I woke up this morning from a hangover that I was still recovering from, but I felt compelled to now. "What do you drink?"

"I'll take a Jack and Coke."

Turning to the bartender. "Can I get a Jack and Coke for my friend and my usual please?" The bartender smiled and nodded. Then got to work on our drinks.

I glanced at Blake. His back turned to me. He was looking at the crowd dancing. *I wonder if he liked to dance.* His silhouette showed off an athletic, toned build. He wasn't grooving to the beat of the music. *He either had no rhythm or hated dancing.* My lips slightly curved up to a small smile at that thought.

The bartender handed me the drinks. "Enjoy."

I gave Blake his drink. He raised his glass up. "To us running into one another. Cheers."

I followed his gesture and raised mine. "To us running into one another. Cheers."

Then our glasses lightly touched as we toasted. I took a sip of my wine.

Blake leaned in. "I'm ready for a tour when you are."

I gestured with my hand for Blake to follow me. "Come on. Let's go."

BLUE VELVET LOUNGE wasn't a large venue, but we somehow ended up walking around, refilling our drinks several times, and talk about the lounge and living in LA for over an hour. When we reached my office in the back of the venue, the party had already ended and my staff were finishing up their cleaning routine. I'm not sure how many drinks we had, but I was super buzzed and felt good, probably because Blake was still here with me. *He was so sexy.*

Sitting on the opposite side of my desk, Blake gazed at me with a smoldering look. The desk between us—the only thing keeping me from doing anything I may regret. *I just wanted to rip his clothes off and jump his bones.* Not sure if that was me or the alcohol making those suggestions, but it had been a while since

I slept with someone. Glenn broke my heart this morning and this may be the remedy to heal it.

A knock on the door startled us. Britney opened the door, surprised to see Blake in the office with me. She smiled wide as she looked at me, then Blake, and me again.

"Boss, we're all done here. Did you need anything before I go? I sent the staff home already."

"No, I'm good. Thanks, Britney. You did a great job with this event."

Britney's smile faded and she looked a bit worried. "*We* did a great job with this event. Will you be okay driving home tonight?"

"I'm good, Brit. We'll be leaving soon anyway. Drive home safely." I gave her a look of reassurance.

"Alright boss, I'll lock the front door on my way out. Have a good night!" She gave an amused smirk.

"Thank you, doll. Good night."

As soon as the door closed, Blake turned, facing me. "You're so damn gorgeous, you know that?" His hazel-green eyes were vivid and energized.

I got up from my chair and walked to the office door.

His gaze followed me. "So, is this a cue that we're leaving?"

"No. I just needed to get up." *I can't believe I'm about to do this, but I can't resist him.* I turned the latch and locked the door. "Well, I think you're so damn sexy yourself, sir."

Blake raised one eyebrow. His eyes fixated on me as I headed back to my desk. This time I sat on the edge of it, right in front of Blake. Crossing my legs and folding my hands on my lap, I noticed his eyes shift. "I'm not looking for anything serious."

Blake's gaze was intense as he looked down at my legs then slowly made his way back up to my eyes. Blake placed his hands on the desk, each hand brushing the side of my thighs. He stood up. "Neither am I."

His eyes captivated me, I couldn't stop staring at them. As his face got closer to mine, my heartbeat sped up and I was breathless. If I wanted to run away, I couldn't... and I wouldn't even think about doing that. Blake cupped my jaw, then his mouth pressed lightly against mine, surprising me with a gentle kiss. I opened my lips and he deepened the kiss. His tongue explored the depths of my mouth. The slickness of his tongue brushed against mine sending shivers of desire through my body.

I uncrossed my legs and opened them wide enough as an invitation for Blake to move in closer. Draping my arms around his neck, I pulled him toward me as our tongues continued to collide into each other's. Blake moved in closer as I wrapped my legs around his hips. I could feel the heat of his body against mine and the growing pressure of his length wanting to protrude out of his jeans. My sex throbbed at the feel of his bulge, making my lace thong wet with need.

Starting from below my ear, he left a trail of kisses down my neck. Then pulled away from me. My legs released their hold around his waist.

"Did you want to do this?" he said.

"Yes, I want you. I want to feel you inside me."

"When was the last time you were tested? I was tested last week and I'm clean."

Trying to catch my breath. "I went to my doctor a month ago and I'm on the pill. I got tested and I'm also clean."

"That's what I liked to hear."

Blake returned to my neck, kissing down the side and then moved on to my décolletage. Tilting my head back, it gave him access to more of me. He reached for the bottom of my dress and pulled the stretchy material over my head, exposing my undergarments.

"Damn!" he whispered in my ear. "You're absolutely gorgeous." He gawked at the black lace bra I had on. His hands reached behind my back and unhooked it. Removing my bra, the cool draft from my office air vent swept over my breasts, giving my skin tiny goose bumps and making my light brown nipples hard. Blake examined my breasts, then cupped one boob with his hand and squeezed as he devoured the other with his mouth. He sucked on the tip, then alternated between flicking and encircling the areola with his tongue. I moaned.

I clenched his shirt, unbuttoned it quickly, and he shrugged it off his muscular arms. "It's your turn." My hands felt the smooth skin and hard muscles of his chest. Then they trailed down toward his waist, my fingers following the deep grooves of his abs. I reached down and grabbed the bulge at the front of his jeans. Blake shuddered. We kissed wildly as I undid his belt, pants button, and unzipped his pants. I wanted to release the beast out into the wild. Pulling the elastic on the waist of his boxer briefs, I stuck my hand inside. *Oh my!* I grabbed his cock and stroked it from the base to the tip to get a sense of his size before I took it out. He groaned as I continued to stroke the silkiness of his length.

His hand brushed up my thigh and covered the front of my lace thong.

"You're so wet." His voice deep and low.

I moaned with his touch on my sex.

Blake grasped the elastic waist of my thong and pushed it down as I stood up from the desk, only leaving me with my high heels on. He gazed at me from head to toe, revealing a raw, animalistic need in his eyes.

He devoured my breast with his mouth again, sucking on the erect nipple. His finger grazed my swollen clit, getting my pussy wetter with his touch. He applied some pressure on my clit with his thumb and slowly rubbed in a circular motion. *Oh fuck!* I squirmed then arched my back. He rubbed a little faster. I whimpered. Blake placed his middle finger into my entrance and pulled out.

I let go of his hard length when he pushed his middle finger back in and then out again. I shifted on the desk.

"You like that, beautiful?"

"Yes," I said breathy and aroused.

He slid his finger all the way into my slick sex. I let out a cry. He went a little faster, gliding his finger in and out with a swiftness. I was almost to the edge, then he stopped.

"Not yet... I want to feel your tight, wet pussy against my cock." Blake removed the rest of his clothing. His muscles flexed, showing every inch of muscle he had on his sexy, toned body.

"You're fucking hot!" My eyes scanned every inch of his body, lowering my gaze to his v-lines, and then focused on his erection. *Wow!* Hope his package will fit inside me.

"Do you have a condom?" he asked.

"No, but I'm on the pill so it's fine if you're good with that. I want to feel you... skin-to-skin." I breathed heavily.

"Of course, beautiful."

I sat on the edge of my desk and spread my legs open, my elbows bent, propping me up to stabilize me. Blake grabbed onto my waist and moved closer in. His erection grazed against my wet folds and clit. Then he thrust into my opening.

I gasped when his thickness filled my pussy. It felt amazing. I wrapped my legs around his waist.

He growled as he plunged further in. "Fuck! You're so tight... ahh... and so wet."

"Ohhh... fuuuck!" I cried out.

Blake thrust harder, deeper, and faster, getting me closer to reaching my breaking point and exploding onto his thick, hard cock. My breasts bounced with every plunge. I propped up on my hands, arching my back as a surge of pleasure went through my body.

My moans got louder with every penetration. He groaned,

sweat beading on his forehead and chest. Our gaze only focusing on one another. Never breaking.

"Ohhh... I'm going to come soon," I screamed. "Oh fuck!" I gripped on to his broad shoulders, digging my nails into his skin.

Blake grunted and bucked faster. "Fuccck! I'm coming."

Our bodies jerked as we reached the edge of ecstasy. I let out a loud moan with my release and held on to Blake. He groaned and gave one last push inside me to empty himself. Blake looked spent as his body went limp onto mine, lowering us onto the desk.

After a few minutes of lying there, holding one another, Blake got up and cleaned himself up. He didn't look at me when it was over. He put his clothes back on as if what just happened didn't affect him at all and I wasn't there. This was my first time with another man. No cuddling, no talking, nothing happened. I looked away from him, embarrassed. *Did I do something wrong? Was I that bad?* I got up and started to get dressed as well. "I... I need to finish up here and lock up the lounge."

I looked up at the sound of the office door closing. Blake left without a word.

I guess we both got what we wanted from each other. Then why do I feel like shit?

7

ARIANNA

Tossing and turning in bed, I couldn't sleep. I replayed what happened between Blake and I over and over again. *What just happened?* I felt horrible and used, but being with Blake felt so amazing and electrifying, definitely different from having sex with Glenn. I've never felt that way with Glenn before. *Blake just felt right.* I normally don't sleep with guys that I first meet, well, except for this guy. *I don't know what came over me.* I was just dumped by my longtime boyfriend that afternoon and I'm sleeping with the first guy I met. *He was my rebound.* How can this stranger make me feel so sexy yet feel so cheap? I told Blake that I didn't want anything serious. *It was true.* He said that he felt the same.

I reflected back on my relationship with Glenn. He loved me... or so I thought. He had made comments throughout the years we were together that hurt me. Many times, he made me feel worthless, telling me that no other man will love me because of my looks and my weight... and I believed him. Every time he broke up with me, I ran after him, wanting him back. I couldn't let go. I loved him. Was that really love? Or was I that stupid and naive?

Even though being with Blake felt amazing, it also felt like he only had one thing on his agenda. He just wanted to have sex with me, and I gave it to him. *Glenn was right.* Guys like Glenn and Blake are attracted to women like me because they think I'm an easy target. Heat rushed to my head as I glared at the ceiling, pursing my lips to a thin line. I am not easy, a slut, and someone who sleeps around. I'm *not* going to let that happen again with any other guy. I wished Mama was here to guide me. Frustrated with all my thoughts, tears slid down my cheeks and onto my pillow. I cried myself to sleep.

NOT SURE WHAT time I actually fell asleep, I woke up at noon mentally and physically exhausted. I did my best to get out of bed to start my day.

Sitting by the kitchen island and drinking my coffee, I scrolled through my emails and texts that I received since last night. I had a few missed calls from Lolo Tony. I didn't know if I had the strength to talk to him right now, especially if he wanted to discuss work and the "investment" he bought me for my birthday.

Ring. Ring. Ring.

Speaking of which.

"Hi Lolo Tony. How are you?"

"Arianna, anak, you're finally up."

"Yes, Lolo. Sorry I missed your calls. It was a long night." *It was also a night full of passion and hot sex with a gorgeous man.* I smirked at the thought of what happened last night with Blake.

"Oh, how was your event?"

"It went well."

"I didn't expect anything less from you. Glad it was successful. The reason I called is that I wanted to talk to you about the investment opportunity that we got you for your birthday."

"Okay, Lolo. What is this investment you're excited to tell me about?"

"So I was talking to Glenn about his new job—"

"What? You were talking to Glenn? Why?" *Oh my God!*

"When he got hired for his new job, he called to tell me. He said he was going to tell your dad as well."

"Okay... and..." My voice giving away that I'm wary about where this conversation was headed.

"Glenn explained to me about hockey and about the National Hockey League. He also said that owning a sports team would be a good investment and opportunity for our family."

"What are you saying, Lolo?"

"I bought the San Francisco Storm hockey team, and I would like to give it to you as your birthday gift."

What? A sports team? I had no words. I'm stunned by this generosity.

"Arianna? Anak? Are you there?"

"Yes. I'm still here... I'm just trying to process everything... umm... so you want *me* to be the owner of a hockey team and run it?"

"Syempre, ang aking magandang apo. Of course, my beautiful granddaughter. I know that with the help of Glenn, you will make our hockey team successful."

Shit! Should I tell him that Glenn and I are not together? Ugh. My family loves Glenn. He definitely turned on his charm to impress the men in my family, if they only knew.

"Thanks, Lolo Tony, but I'll need to think about this. I don't know anything about hockey—"

"That's why you have Glenn. He can help—"

"We're no longer together."

"What happened? Why are you two not together anymore? What did you do?" The tone of his voice became serious. He sounded upset.

"Why would you think it was my fault that we're not together?" In my culture, it was not good to talk back to your elders, but I didn't consider it talking back, merely asking a question with a bit of sass.

"I'm sorry, anak. I didn't mean to put the blame on you. I know that you're a good girl. With your job, you're always busy. You probably didn't have time for him and that's why you two are not together anymore."

"Lolo, it was mutual. We felt that we were drifting apart." Even though Glenn didn't treat me well, I didn't want my family to think any less of him. Glenn was part of my family for twelve years.

"That's too bad, Arianna. I still want to give you the San Francisco Storm and have you run the organization. Even without Glenn, I think you'll do a great job. You're a hard worker."

"Lolo Tony, I appreciate this opportunity, but please let me think about it. It's a lot to process and it would demand more of my time. I don't know."

"I wouldn't be giving this team to you if I didn't think you could do it, but I'll wait... hopefully not too long."

"Thanks, Lolo. I'll give you an answer sometime next week."

"That's okay. I can wait. Love you, anak."

"Love you too. Please tell Lola Lynn that I said hi and I love her too."

"I will, Arianna. Take care."

"Bye Lolo."

I couldn't believe the opportunity my grandfather offered me. What the hell was he thinking? A sports team as my birthday gift? I didn't know anything about hockey or any sport for that matter. Why doesn't he give it to Kuya Eric or my other cousins? I really don't get it. I spent the majority of my time working at the lounge. Now that the lounge is getting business, how am I supposed to handle both?

So many questions raced through my head. My head was throbbing and it wasn't the lack of caffeine. I couldn't focus. Just thinking about this made me nauseous and anxious. One thing for sure was for that brief moment, it helped me to forget about Blake and Glenn.

8

BLAKE

I woke up with a headache and a slight hangover. Waiting for my coffee to brew in the kitchen, I popped two Advil in my mouth and downed a glass of water. How much did I have to drink last night? *Oh yeah, last night I was with Arianna.* Images of the gorgeous, voluptuous woman I spent the night with appeared in my mind, and soon my arousal appeared through my shorts. She was different from other women I had slept with. There was a definite connection between us. She didn't seem to care who I was. Thinking about that, she probably didn't know I was a professional hockey player. But it didn't matter.

I was only looking for a hookup last night. I needed to release all that I had pent-up inside, emotionally and physically. Being with Arianna did not feel like another random hookup though. The more I replayed that passionate night with the sensual woman, the more I craved to see her again. My dick felt the same way too. It started to get hard and pulsated for her touch and her sex on it. I put my hand inside my shorts and started to stroke my length as I thought about Arianna. Then I remembered what I saw after we were done that made me regret everything. I let go of my manhood and the urge to please myself passed. How could I be so stupid as to have sex with a woman who was clearly not single? She told me she was single, but who in their right mind would not be with her? She was successful and gorgeous as hell. I also mentioned to her that I wasn't looking for anything serious. *So why was I so upset about this hookup?* It's not like I was looking to get tied down, but still... she lied to me.

I can still see that photo of Arianna with another man sitting on a shelf beside her office desk. He had his arms around her and was kissing her cheek... that sexy woman that I could not stop thinking about. I only managed to see his side profile in the picture, and he looked vaguely familiar; however, I couldn't pinpoint where I knew him from. He was probably a celebrity. We lived in LA, so the chances of him being someone famous would be very likely. She looked very happy in the photograph with her boyfriend, husband, or whoever he was to her. Arianna didn't wear a ring from my recollection so maybe she wasn't married. I couldn't remember the little details, but I can certainly recall the dress she wore and what she had on underneath. Last night, her eyes told me that she was single. That she wanted *me* and nobody else. Although, if we were just looking to have some fun, then why did it feel like more than *just sex*?

My thoughts were interrupted by a phone call. I grabbed my cell phone off the counter and saw that it was *Dad*. Dad always has a way of interrupting my life during the most inopportune moments. The sight of his name calmed my hard-on quickly, not to mention the fact that I had become bitter about last night's events and soon my flesh softened.

"Hey, Dad. What's going on? How are you?"

"I should be asking you the same thing. I've been calling and texting you since last night. I wanted to speak with you. I watched the game on TV last night."

"Sorry, Dad. It was a rough night and I didn't want to talk to anyone after the game." *Actually, it was just him I didn't want to talk to.*

There was a brief silence followed by a heavy sigh.

"Blake, you got ejected from the game last night. What the hell were you thinking?" Dad asked with disappointment.

"Well—"

"Let me tell you. You weren't thinking. Goaltenders do *not* get ejected from games unless something major happens, and you did just that. What do you have to say?" Dad interrupted, his voice became upset and angry.

"I'm sorry, Dad."

"That's all you have to say?" he snapped.

"What else do you want to hear?" Raising my voice. "I'm sorry that I lost my temper. I'm sorry that I got removed from the game. I'm sorry that I kicked the crap out of that player."

"Don't you raise your voice at me, Blake Collins. Don't be stupid. I didn't raise a son that talked back to his father."

I didn't know what to say except, "Yes sir."

"I also didn't raise a son to be a failure. You're a Collins. A legacy in the Crusaders. You need to get your fucking act together, Blake. Another stunt like what happened last night could cost you your career. Do you understand that you can be suspended from playing altogether? Get that into your fucking head!"

"Yes, sir," I said through clenched teeth as I tightened my grip on my phone.

"I hope the next time I watch your game, you'll be playing all three periods."

"I'll do my best."

"I certainly hope so. So far this season your best hasn't been good enough. I'll talk to you again soon."

"Bye Dad." I rolled my eyes and shook my head. That man is a jerk and obviously has no love for me. I'm surprised that he even has a heart and love for my mom.

I DECIDED to go for a jog this morning to burn the anger and energy I had suppressed since my conversation with Dad ended. My knee was achy, most likely from all the action I had from the game and with Arianna yesterday, but I decided to limit my use of pain meds. With my knee throbbing, I motivated myself to push through and keep moving. Things seemed better before I got injured. I was taking home a different woman weekly, I was partying and having fun, and I helped win games. I worked hard and played harder.

A mile into the run, my knee pain got worse. I stopped and was determined to walk off the pain. I changed my course and headed back to my house. I couldn't even complete the damn full course I used to run often. Maybe Dad was right. I am a failure and a disappointment. But at least I'm still playing hockey, right? That seemed to be all I had going for me.

9

ARIANNA

I got to work early Saturday morning to catch up on missing a week of work from the emotional and physical hangover I endured last week from JB's event, the breakup with Glenn, and my passionate night with Blake. Sitting in my office, I scrolled through emails and flipped through a pile of paperwork I had on my desk. A light tap on my office door got my attention. I looked up and smiled when I saw it was my lovely assistant.

"Morning, Britney."

"Good morning, Miss Santos. I got your usual from Starbucks this morning. Hope you didn't have your coffee yet." Britney handed me the iced coffee.

How does this girl have so much energy in the mornings, especially when she was always working long hours?

"Thanks, doll. It's much needed this morning. How did you know I was here already?"

"Umm, your social media, duh." Britney let out a laugh. "You posted a pic in your Instagram story and I recognized your office decor in the background. I thought you could use the company since you were out of commission for the last week.

Are you okay?" She raised an eyebrow. "I wanted to ask you last week on the night of JB's event, but didn't want to kill the vibe, what happened with Glenn? Wasn't he supposed to help us out?"

"Well..." I didn't know whether I should say anything to Britney. I trusted her with my business, but I haven't really discussed my personal life with her. She's met Glenn, but never really talked to him. She tended to leave when he was around. "Glenn broke up with me earlier that day—"

"What?! No wonder you were hanging out with someone else. I was thinking that if Glenn came by, he would have been pissed."

"Glenn told me he met someone else."

"I knew he was an asshole—"

"What do you mean, Brit? You never really talked to him." My eyes narrowed on her and she squirmed in her seat. "Britney, why do you think he's an asshole?"

"A few years ago, on the day of my interview with you, I came into the lounge. I sat at the bar waiting for you, and Glenn sat right next to me." Britney swallowed nervously. "He complimented my attire, then asked if I was seeing anyone. I told him that I wasn't interested and that I was there for an interview..." She looked down at her hands which held her cup of joe. "Glenn told me that he knew the owner of Blue Velvet and he would put a good word in to the boss if I went out to dinner with him. Then he put his hand on my thigh."

My gaze went from confused to livid. Not toward Britney, but at the man I gave my everything to. I clenched my jaw at the thought of Glenn hitting on other women while we were together. *That bastard.*

"I'm so sorry, Miss Santos, that I didn't tell you sooner... I was scared to lose my job, especially since you decided to hire me. You're my boss and I respect you. I would never hurt you intentionally."

"I know... I know. Why didn't I see it before? How could I be so stupid?" I wanted to bang my head against my desk. Instead, I just put my head down on my arms on the table.

"Miss Santos, I've never been in a serious relationship before. I've heard that when you're in love, sometimes you're blind to everything else in the relationship. Maybe that's why you didn't see it or wanted to believe it?"

My head slowly rose up and I shook my head in disbelief. *Mama said the same thing before she passed.* "I guess so. I don't know anymore."

"On a lighter note, I saw you with that hot guy the night of JB's event. How did that go? I didn't mean to interrupt you guys before I left."

"He was so amazing!" I grinned, thinking of what Blake and I did on this desk after hours. "And as usual, I left alone at the end of the night." I decided to skip the details of my steamy night with Blake. I already felt stupid as fuck because of Glenn and being blindsided by what a complete jerk he was. I didn't want Britney to judge me even more if she found out that I slept with Blake right away after my breakup.

Holding my coffee up to Britney, I quickly changed the subject. "Thanks again, Brit." I sipped on the iconic green straw. That first taste of iced coffee hit the spot.

"No prob!" Sitting across from me, Britney looked more at ease after telling me her experience with Glenn. "So what do you need me to work on this morning, boss lady?"

I gave Britney a project to work on that recapped JB's Birthday Bash event. While giving her all the details of the project, I got interrupted by my cell phone ringing.

Who could be calling me at seven-thirty a.m. on a Saturday? I looked down at the caller ID and saw that it was my dad. "Hey Brit, you don't need to leave the office, but I need to take this call." I didn't expect the phone call from my dad to be anything too personal. He was probably going to remind me of our monthly family dinner coming up.

Britney nodded, multitasking between going through the paperwork I had given her and sipping her coffee.

"Hi Daddy. How are you? I haven't spoken to you in a few days."

"Arianna, anak, I need you to come home as soon as you're able to. Your Lolo Tony—"

"What about Lolo Tony? Is he okay? I talked to him last week."

"He had a major stroke and is in the hospital right now. Your Lola Lynn called 911 very early this morning."

"Oh my God! Which hospital is he at? How is he?" I felt like my heart just stopped and the wind was knocked out of me. My eyes opened wide as I gasped to catch my breath.

Britney looked up from what she was doing, her smile fading, and a look of concern replaced the happiness that was there a minute ago.

"He's at Sequoia Grove Hospital, and in the ICU. The specialists and doctors are running tests to see how much the stroke affected his brain."

"Okay, Daddy. I'll go home now to pack some things and take the first flight to SFO. I'll text you my flight info as soon as I know."

"I'll ask your Kuya Eric to pick you up. See you soon, anak. Love you. Be safe."

"Thank you, Daddy. Love you too."

I hung up the phone. Tears welled up in my eyes. I couldn't believe that Lolo was in the hospital. I literally just spoke with him recently. He was giving me a hockey team as a birthday gift. How could he have a stroke? He always took good care of himself. I couldn't believe it.

"Hey, boss. Are you alright? What happened?"

"Britney, it's my grandfather. My dad said he had a stroke."
Still in shock from the news.

"I'm so sorry to hear that. Please let me know if you need anything from me."

"Actually, I do. I need to leave and go home to San Francisco. I'm not sure when I'll be back. I need you to watch over the lounge and take care of things for me."

"Of course. I can do that. I'll make sure things run smoothly."

"I trust you, Brit. I know you won't let me down. I'll be available by phone and video call if you need me."

"Thanks, Miss Santos. I hope your grandpa has a speedy recovery."

I quickly stuffed my work bag with my laptop, planner, and some paperwork. Grabbing my purse, work bag, and cell phone, I looked around to make sure I didn't forget anything. I gave Britney a hug before leaving the Blue Velvet Lounge.

"I'll keep you updated. Bye."

UGH! *Come on!* I don't know if driving myself to the airport would have gotten me to the destination quicker than being in this ride-share. I kept the anxiety building up inside to myself, and remained quiet in the back seat of the car. I booked my flight to San Francisco for two o'clock. We have another five miles left to get to LAX. I needed to get to the airport in an hour or I'll miss my flight. Why does it always happen that when you're in a hurry, it felt like it took forever to get where you needed to go? I even left my house a little earlier, but this LA traffic is no joke. I texted my dad my flight information.

After thirty minutes of bumper to bumper traffic, the driver dropped me off in front of the airline check-in area. Going through security was quick and I finally made it to my assigned gate... just in time for boarding. I was greeted by the gate attendant who scanned my boarding pass on my phone. At the end of the passenger boarding bridge, the friendly flight crew welcomed me on board the plane. I found my seat in the first-class section of the aircraft. Although the flight only took an hour and a half, I preferred to have a quieter and more comfortable space on the plane.

Flying was not my first choice in modes of transportation. There's something that freaks me out when I'm on the plane. I took out a small orange bottle from my purse. I asked the flight attendant for a bottled water. When she returned with my drink, I popped half an Ativan into my mouth and guzzled the water to make sure the little white pill slid all the way down my throat. Inhaling and exhaling a few deep breaths helped calm my jitters. A few minutes later, we took off into the bright blue sky at the right moment my anti-anxiety medication started to ease my anxiousness.

"Kuya!" I gave Eric a tight hug as soon as I saw him at the terminal waiting for me. Dressed in a T-shirt, jeans, and a San Francisco Storm baseball cap, he held a sign that said 'Santos' on it. "What's up with the sign?" Pointing at it, I let out a laugh.

"It's been a while since I've seen you, Ari. I didn't know whether you still remembered what I looked like. Plus, Dad said I needed to pick you up, so I wanted to give you the full 'chauffeur' experience."

"Dude! It hasn't been that long. You missed the last family dinner when I came up here. What was the reason again?" I looked at my big brother with a smirk. "Oh that's right, you said it was because you had a business thing to attend... hmm, but when I checked Instagram, I saw that you were on a date! Jerk! Left me alone with our relatives!" I raised an eyebrow and glared at him.

"Oh, Ari! I've missed you, little sis!" Eric laughed out loud. "Let's go before I get charged for the parking." Eric grabbed the luggage handle away from my hand and started pulling it.

I looped my arm around his and tried to keep up with his quick strides. "You haven't changed a bit. You're still cheap as fuck." I nudged his side with my elbow and smiled widely. Being with Kuya Eric felt like I hadn't left home at all. Eric and I were never that close growing up until Mama passed away. Daddy had him when he was still in high school before meeting Mama in college. Eric's biological mom didn't want the responsibility of taking care of him, so Daddy took sole custody of Eric, and Lolo Tony and Lola Lynn helped raise him while Daddy was in school. Mama loved Eric as if he was her own child.

After a few minutes, we found Eric's car and went straight to Sequoia Grove Hospital where Lolo Tony was.

"Kuya, how's Lolo doing? Did the doctors say anything yet?"

"Still the same as this morning. He's not talking much and is sleeping a lot. The doctors are running a bunch of tests on him. He is paralyzed on one side of his body."

"I'm scared. I don't want to lose him."

"I know, Ari. We all feel the same."

TWENTY MINUTES LATER, we arrived at the hospital and found my family sitting in the waiting room on the main floor. Lolo Tony was in the ICU on the fourth floor, and they only allowed up to two visitors at a time. I greeted Lola Lynn, Daddy, and all my relatives and family friends that came to visit Lolo. Many of these people I haven't seen in a very long time and the first thing that came out of their mouths were 'Arianna, dalaga na. You're a young lady now and getting older. When are you going to get married and have kids?' or 'Wow Arianna. You're getting *healthy*.' It's my relatives' way of saying I'm getting old and too thick. As much as I wanted to talk back, I don't want to be rude to the older Filipino generation, so I just laughed and told them that it's great to see them too.

After greeting twenty-five people in the waiting room, it was my turn to go up to see Lolo Tony. Daddy and Kuya Eric asked if I wanted one of them to go with me, but I declined. I wanted to visit Lolo alone. I took the elevator to the fourth floor, inhaling and exhaling deeply and preparing myself mentally and emotionally for what to expect when I saw my grandfather. I checked in with the nurse and she guided me to where Lolo's room was.

I noticed an older gentleman that I didn't recognize, sitting next to his bed facing the door. He stood up as soon as he saw me at the entrance of the room. He was dressed very professionally, wearing a dark suit and a striped, burgundy tie. I overheard the man tell my grandfather, "Tony, you're a strong man and I know you'll recover quickly. We want you to come back soon to watch your team play."

The tall, handsome man with salt and pepper hair stopped in front of me and smiled. "You must be Arianna Santos, Tony's granddaughter."

"Yes, that's correct. I'm sorry, but you are?"

Sticking out his hand, he said, "I'm Elliott Reynolds. I'm the general manager of the San Francisco Storm. Your grandfather has told me so much about you and how great you would be at running the organization."

"Oh, nice to meet you, sir." I shook his hand. "I'm not sure what my grandfather has told you, but I haven't made a decision yet on whether I will run the hockey organization or not."

"I see. Well, Miss Santos, don't wait too long to give your answer. From what I heard, I'm sure you'll be as great as your grandfather said." Elliott handed me his business card.

"*Miss Santos* is too formal. You can call me Arianna. I appreciate your kind words, sir. I'll let you know as soon as I make my decision." I tucked his card in my purse.

"Please, call me Elliott. *Sir* is too formal." He smiled and gave me a wink.

My cheeks warmed up. I walked closer to Lolo's bed, hoping to give Elliott the hint that I wanted time with my grandfather. "Thank you, Elliott, for visiting my grandpa. Again, it was nice to meet you."

"It was my pleasure." Elliott walked out the door, then stopped and turned around to face me. "Hope we will be able to work together or at least see each other again soon." With a grin, he turned around and walked away.

I grabbed a chair and sat down next to Lolo's hospital bed. He was sound asleep with the use of an oxygen machine as well as an IV sending fluids into his arm. I held Lolo Tony's hand, closed my eyes, and said a little prayer to myself. I also asked God not to take this man too soon and to give him the strength to recover.

Feeling a squeeze on my hand, I looked up to see Lolo staring at me. He struggled with his words.

"Ari." He managed to slur my name. One corner of his lip curled up to a half-smile due to his semi-paralysis.

"Hi Lolo." I gave him a small tight-lipped smile. "Do you need anything right now?"

He looked at me with worried eyes. A minute later, he said "no."

"Lolo, I'll be here for you and Lolo Lynn if you need me. I'm not going back home to LA anytime soon, not until you get discharged to go home and have recovered." I gently tightened my hold on his hand, hoping to provide him some reassurance. "If you need anything right now, please let me help you."

It took some time to get a response from him, but he was able to give a breathy "okay" from his lips.

Seeing my grandfather in this physical and mental state

made me feel so helpless, but I knew what I needed to do to help him out during this time. "Lolo, I know you're in no condition to work right now, and I wouldn't want you to work unless you were one-hundred-percent better. So I've decided that I will accept your offer to own and run the hockey organization." I'm not sure if he can process or understand all the information I just blurted out, so I rephrased what I said slowly and simpler. "Lolo, I will accept your offer to run the hockey team."

My grandpa just stared at me with a blank look on his face. *I wonder if he knew what I was talking about.*

Then he smiled. "Thank... you... anak."

AN HOUR LATER, Daddy came up to Lolo's room to check up on us.

"Hi Daddy."

"Ari, how's he doing?"

"The same." I tried to give Daddy a smile, but I couldn't. I felt so emotionally drained.

"Why don't you go back downstairs to be with the rest of the family? I'll stay with him."

"Alright." I bent down to give Lolo Tony a kiss on the forehead before leaving his room, then gave my father a kiss on his cheek. "I'll see you later, Daddy."

Downstairs in the main floor waiting area, I sat next to my cousin Jessa, who sat across from her brother, Christian, and Kuya Eric. I gave my summary of my visit with Lolo and who I met when I arrived at the room.

"Yeah, we've met Elliott when Lolo bought the Storm. He seemed like a cool guy," Kuya said.

Eric and the rest of our family were the first to know when Lolo purchased the San Francisco Storm. They also knew that our grandfather wanted to hand the reins over to me.

Jessa smiled. She leaned closer and whispered in my ear, "He's not that bad looking either."

"Dude. Really?" Christian sent a disgusted look toward Jessa. "So, anyway. Ari, have you decided what to do about Lolo's offer yet?"

They all looked at me, waiting for my answer. I swallowed the knot in my throat. "I did make a decision." I took a deep breath in and exhaled sharply. "You're looking at the new owner of the San Francisco Storm."

They clapped, hugged, and congratulated me causing everyone else in the waiting room to stare at us with all the commotion we were making.

Eric placed his hand on my shoulder and had a huge grin on his face. "We knew you would agree to it, and so did Lolo Tony. That's why he put your name on the contract as an owner already."

"What?!" I was in complete shock. "Why?"

"Because our Lolo wanted to give it to you as your birthday present. He knew that you wouldn't say no to him."

"And with the help of Glenn, your team will be a force to be reckoned with," Christian added on.

"What do you mean with the help of Glenn?"

Christian hesitated to give me an answer. "You know Lolo talked to Glenn before purchasing the team, right? Since Glenn knows a lot about the sport—"

"Yeah, Lolo told me. So?" I interrupted, irritated and annoyed hearing my ex's name.

"Since you and Glenn have been together for a super long time and will probably get married soon, Lolo thought it would be good for you and Glenn to run the team together—"

"Well, that's not going to happen. Glenn and I broke up. He left me for someone else, so..." I snapped.

There was a sudden awkward silence in the room.

"I'm sorry, Ari. We didn't know." Jessa draped her arms around me from where she sat and gave me a squeeze.

"I'll be fine. I don't need Glenn in my life anymore. Plus, having *my* team here in the city has its advantages... it guarantees that I won't be running into him around LA."

10

BLAKE

"I 'm so happy to hear your voice, honey. How are you?"

"I'm doing pretty crappy, Mom. I just wanted to hear your voice. I've missed you." Hearing my mom's voice felt so comforting. I wished she was close by. She was always ready to give me advice when I needed it.

"Blake, we miss you too. What's wrong? Is there something I can do to help you?" Mom asked. A tinge of worry and concern was in her voice. "Are you having girlfriend problems?"

"Mom, I'm fine. I don't have a girlfriend and I'm not dating anyone. I'm just tired. I think it's all the traveling."

"You're on the road?"

"Yes, we're on the east coast right now."

"I don't know how athletes do it. Your dad always complained about being on the road a lot. It seems so tiring."

"It can be."

"Oh Blake, remember, I don't want you to get sick…" Here it comes, what my mother always says. "Please make sure to get lots of rest and hydrate." I smiled and mimicked those words as my mom said it. Every phone call usually ended with that. She hated it when I stayed up late and when I didn't drink enough water. She's a true believer that water and sleeping well worked wonders on the body.

"Thanks, Mom. I will."

"Your dad's here and would like to talk to you."

"That's fine, Mom. I love you."

"I love you too, Blake," Mom said sweetly.

There was a muffled sound. Then a deep, gruffy voice came on the other end of the receiver. "Hello."

"Hey, Dad."

"Blake, I've been watching your games. What the hell is wrong with you?"

"Well—"

"I'm not done talking yet."

"Alright, Dad," I whispered.

"The way you've been playing is definitely not smart goal-tending. It's ludicrous. You're being stupid. You need to man up and play like I've taught you."

"Yes, sir."

"Don't you have a game tomorrow night?"

"Yes, sir."

"Well, I suggest you listen to your mother and get some rest."

"Okay, Dad. Good—"

Click. Dad hung up the phone mid-sentence.

Of course he hung up the phone. He never wanted to hear me out. He just watched and criticized the way I played. I took a deep breath in and let out the heaviness that was bearing down on my chest. *Argh!* I wanted to punch something, but I just kept the aggression in and tried to forget how much of an asshole my father was.

I got a drink of water and got ready for bed, an hour earlier than I normally did... finally taking my mother's advice.

It was day seven of the Crusader's road trip. Planes, buses, hotels. That's the life we lived being on the road. Being away from home ice sucked, and we've had a rough start to our away games. We lost all three road games we've played so far, and with each of those games we lost, I was ejected during the third period for a major violation. I haven't been able to find my groove and play like how I normally played when on home ice. The vibe of these arenas were completely different and it threw me off. *It can also be that I had Arianna on my mind. It's been over a week since I met her (and slept with her), and she's left quite an impression on me.*

Tonight, we were playing in New York against the Scorpions. They were ranked number one in the Eastern Conference and had a ten-game winning streak so far. If you were to bet on this game in Vegas or Atlantic City, the odds of the Crusaders to win this game is twenty-to-one. Being in a three-game losing streak had a lot of pressure on us. We wanted to win. We needed to win.

We arrived at New York's arena this evening and we all got ready like we usually did before each game. Taping the blades on my sticks and suiting up with all my gear, I put my earbuds in to hype myself up pregame. Hockey was not only a physical sport, but it was also mental as well. I needed to get into the right headspace before the game started.

Fifteen minutes later, arena staff informed us that it was time for pregame skate. The Crusaders and I headed to the rink and began our pregame practice and stretching. Meyers and I warmed up and took turns making sure we could freely skate around the crease. The forwards and defensemen worked on their drills of skating, passing, and shooting on goal. When it was my turn to get to the crease, Coach Wilson called me to the bench.

"What's up, Coach?" I moved the cage of my mask up and on top of my head.

Coach handed me his cell phone. "You need to take this call."

Is this a family emergency? My heart sank thinking about it. Then I saw the name on the caller ID: *Sam Cunningham. Oh shit! The general manager of the Crusaders.*

"Hello?"

"Hi, Blake. This is Sam Cunningham. Listen, Blake, we made a trade. You're going to San Francisco. Someone from San Francisco will be calling you. We really liked you, but this is the nature of the game. It's nothing personal."

"Excuse me? Can you repeat what you just said one more time? I didn't quite catch everything. Did you just say I've been traded?" I leaned against the boards in shock. I could not believe what I was hearing on the other end of this phone.

"Yes, you heard correctly. You've been traded to San Francisco. Someone from San Francisco will be calling you and giving you details on your flight to the Bay Area."

"Why?!" I raise my voice. My cheeks heated up as my blood boiled from all the rage I had pent-up inside. I looked up to see Coach Wilson and the assistant coaches watching me. Eyes shifted from the fans behind our bench looking toward me.

"Look, Blake, since your return, you've caused at least seven major penalties as well as a couple misconduct penalties. Keep this up and you will be suspended from the league. *You* should know that goaltenders don't usually get suspended from the league."

"I can't be traded. Doesn't it say that in my contract somewhere?"

"Unfortunately, Blake, your contract does not state anywhere that there is a no-trade clause. As mentioned, it's nothing personal. We wish you the best. Good luck." Then the general manager hung up.

I handed the cell phone back to Coach. When he reached out for the phone, I grabbed his hand and pulled him closer to me, facing him square in the eye. Coach's eyes opened wide. He looked worried. He probably thought I was going to hit him.

In a low voice, I said, "Did you know? Did you know that I was being traded?"

"I just found out today. I don't have anything to do with trades. That's all upper management."

I had nothing to say because I knew Coach was right.

"Blake, good luck."

ON THE WAY to JFK airport from the hotel, I got a phone call from a *Private Number*. It was probably the general manager from the Storm.

I answered the call, "This is Blake."

"Hey, Blake Collins. This is Elliott Reynolds, the GM from the San Francisco Storm. As you know, you've been traded to the Storm and we couldn't be more excited to have you on the team. We arranged a red-eye flight from LAX to SFO tonight. Hope that gives you enough time to get some things from home before coming up here. We also set you up at a nice hotel near the arena. I'll have my assistant email you the details. Any questions?"

"No, sir."

"Alright then. Welcome to the team. See you at practice on Monday."

11

ARIANNA

Kuya Eric dropped me off at my dad's house so I could rest before going back to the hospital to stay with Lolo overnight. My typical Saturday nights were filled with partying in LA, working, and being with Glenn. However, a lot has already changed within the last week and I foresee a lot more changes to the LA lifestyle I was used to happening very soon. With all the commotion with my grandfather being in the hospital, I haven't had a chance to text my best friends. The last time I reached out to them was before the celebrity event at Blue Velvet. My girlfriends were aware of how busy I had been with work, I'm not sure if they knew that I was here in San Francisco. I'm happy for social media though. It kept me in the loop on their lives.

Pulling my cell phone out of my purse, I scrolled through the texts to the group thread I had with Jasmine, Lorelei, and Sasha. It had been a little over a month since we texted in the group. The last message was wishing Sasha a Happy Birthday in September, and now it was early November. I texted the group to see if they were available for a video chat. A lot had been going on and I needed my girls right now. Within a few minutes, all three women responded.

Lorelei text: **Hi Ari! We've missed you, girl! I'm free to video chat.**

Followed by Sasha: **Hey Ari! I'm free too.**

Jasmine was the last one to text: **Hey girl! What's up? We want to see your beautiful face. Hurry up and call us!**

I was surprised that these vibrant women were all available on a Saturday evening instead of out socializing and partying, but the night was still young. I called the girls using the video feature on my phone, and soon my besties were on the screen.

"Hey, ladies! How are you guys?" I asked.

"Arianna! I've missed your face!" Jasmine yelled out. Jasmine was the social butterfly in our group. She would strike up conversations with anyone and say exactly what's on her mind with no filter.

"Hey, Jas! I've missed your face more. I've missed all you girls so much."

Lorelei chimed in, "Hey, Ari! Things have been the same with me. How've you been?" Lorelei is the 'mother' of the group. She took care of us whenever we had problems and whenever we partied too hard and were hungover.

Then Sasha took a turn to speak before I could get a word in. "Hey, girlfriend! We've all been doing well. How's life been with you?" Sasha was the smart and logical one. She thought things through before doing anything and weighed the pros and cons before making decisions. She was finishing up her doctoral degree in social work and would be graduating in the spring.

"Well—"

"Are you back home in the city? I recognize your room," Jasmine interrupted.

"Yeah, I'm home. Lolo Tony had a stroke and is at Sequoia Grove right now."

All the women stopped what they were doing and were speechless. Their eyes wide, their faces showing they're saddened by the news.

"I'm so sorry, Ari. How's Lolo doing?" Sasha asked.

"He's okay. The doctors are running tests to see how much the stroke affected his brain."

"Aww girl. I'm so sorry to hear that. How are you doing?" Lorelei's voice cracked and sounded as if she was about to cry.

"I'm okay. Just needed to talk to you girls. I've missed you all!"

"Oh girl! You know we're here for you," Jasmine stated.

Their eyes showed sincerity and concern for me and Lolo.

"What are your plans for tonight? You guys busy?"

"What's up, Ari?" Sasha asked.

"Want to grab a bite to eat soon? I need to relieve my dad at the hospital right after dinner."

All three women accepted the invitation to go out to dinner, and they wanted to carpool since I was carless. We decided to go to this cute little bistro, *Cafe Rosalinda*, in the Noe Valley neighborhood.

"I'll see you ladies in thirty minutes."

WHILE I WAITED for my friends to pick me up to go to dinner, I reflected back on the visit at the hospital earlier today. I couldn't believe that I told Lolo Tony and my family that I accepted the proposal to be the owner of the San Francisco Storm and run their hockey organization. I didn't really have time to ruminate over this offer after the phone call with my grandfather. But due to Lolo's current medical condition, I wouldn't know what would happen if I decided to say 'no.' According to Kuya Eric, Lolo wouldn't have taken 'no' for an answer. My grandfather insisted on gifting me the ownership so I could manage the San Francisco Storm franchise, and for some reason, he felt I would be a great fit for the job even though I didn't know anything about hockey.

Remembering I had Elliott's card in my purse, I took it out, grabbed my cell phone, and dialed the number listed on the card. After a couple of rings, Elliott answered.

"This is Elliott Reynolds."

"Hi Mr. Reynolds. This is Arianna Santos. We met at the hospital today when you came to vis—"

"Yes, Arianna. How could I forget a beautiful woman like yourself? I told you to call me Elliott." His voice was deep and sensual.

"I apologize, Elliott."

"No need for apologies. How is Tony?"

"Well, there haven't been any changes. He was able to say a few words, but he smiled and that made me happy."

"That's good to hear. I'm sure you didn't call to update me on Tony's status. Your call was a pleasant surprise though. What can I help you with, Arianna?"

"Well, I made my decision and I am now the new owner of the San Francisco Storm."

"That's wonderful news! Congratulations! The team will be very happy when they find out."

"Thank you, Elliott. Since this is effective today, I guess I'll drop by the office on Monday. Will you be available to show me around?"

"Yes, ma'am."

I laughed. "Please don't call me *ma'am*. I'm not that old."

"Definitely not old, but you're my boss now." He chuckled.

"Well, I still don't like being called *ma'am*. That's an order from your new boss." The tone in my voice was playful and flirty. Elliott was easy to converse with.

"Okay, Arianna. I'll see you in a couple days. Have a good night."

"You as well, Elliott. Good night."

I was smiling ear to ear. That short interaction with Elliott had given me all the feels. Maybe it was because he said I was beautiful or because this opportunity was exciting yet terrifying for me.

I received a text from Lorelei that they were in the driveway in front. I put my thoughts of Elliott and the San Francisco Storm aside and prepared myself to spend the much-needed time with my girlfriends.

"WAIT... what?! You're no longer with Glenn *and* you're now the owner of a hockey team? Arianna Santos! Were you ever going to tell us?!" Jasmine sounded as if she was my mother scolding me for doing something I wasn't supposed to be doing.

"Yes! That's why I asked if you all wanted to go out for dinner to catch up." I giggled. "But seriously, I need you guys right now. I'm so stressed with all of this."

Sasha sat on the opposite side from where I was sitting, and I saw that her eyes were focused on something behind Lorelei and me. She was processing all the information. Lorelei turned to me, and by her expression, she knew there was more I needed to add on about my life. Jasmine was still in shock. She was a talker, but grew very quiet.

Lorelei broke the silence. "Okay, Ari, let's start with Glenn. What the hell happened?"

"He left me for someone else."

"We always knew he was an asshole," Jasmine said with hatred in her eyes.

"What do you mean? I thought you all liked him."

"We told you before that if he made you happy, then we're

happy for *you*. He was no good for you, and we told you that, but you continued to stay with him. You two were on-again and off-again for years. You and Glenn fought a lot, and you shed so many tears because of him. How did you expect us to feel?" Lorelei's voice was wobbly so I knew her words were heartfelt.

I knew they all meant well. "I don't want you to feel sorry for me. I should have listened to you guys, but I didn't. Mama warned me about Glenn, but I didn't listen to her either. I'm such an idiot."

"You're definitely not an idiot," Sasha added. "We can't tell you what you need to do with your life. You know that we're here to support you one-hundred-percent."

"I know. I get it and appreciate it. I can't believe how I was blind to how much of a jerk Glenn really was. It makes me so mad that I wasted so many years of my life on *him*."

"Well, girlfriend... now you're free, single, and ready to mingle." Jasmine laughed.

"Yes, I definitely am." I smiled and looked at the girls for reassurance that I would be okay.

"So now you're single and own a hockey team, I'm sure you will find some hot hockey player you can date," Lorelei said with a smirk on her face. "Can you introduce me to a couple of the sexy men on your hockey team? Please and thanks." Lorelei winked.

"Lori, you are too funny!" I laughed. The other two women laughed as well. "And yes, of course, I'll introduce you to the hockey team. I'm going to start on Monday."

"How did you get the Storm anyway?" Sasha had a puzzled look on her face. "Ari, we know you don't know much about sports."

I told them how I obtained Storm ownership. Then we continued laughing and reminiscing about the fun times we had in college from how we all met to where our friendships had taken us to the present. We met in anatomy class where we all were taking our prerequisites to be nurses as encouraged by each of our Filipino families. The only one that succeeded in finishing up nursing school was Lorelei. She definitely followed in her family's footsteps with many of them being nurses. Jasmine, Sasha, and I felt it wasn't the best fit for us. When I couldn't pass any of the science classes, I knew that was a sign that nursing was not for me.

"So there's one other thing I forgot to mention. Remember the big celeb event that was hosted at Blue Velvet a little over a week ago?"

The ladies nodded.

"Well... I kind of had a... one-night stand with one of the guests in the lounge after hours," I said quickly.

"Oh my God, Ari!" Sasha's eyes widened as she stared at me, surprised.

"Tell us all about him. We want to know the details." Jasmine leaned in closer from across the table.

"Alright. His name is Blake. I'm not sure if he was on a pro sports team or if he was just a guest. But his body was... was... like it was made in a lab, like he was Captain America." My cheeks flushed and my body heated up thinking about him. "There was just something about him. I don't know, but it was amazing."

Jasmine, Lorelei, and Sasha smiled at me with the biggest grins on their faces.

"Damn girl! I want to meet this guy... and does he have any friends?" Lorelei joked, but I knew she was a bit serious.

"It was a one-night stand, Lori. I didn't get his number, not even his last name. Now that I'm in San Francisco, I don't think I'll ever see him again. Plus, he just left right after it was all over... didn't even say goodbye."

"What the hell? That's a jerk move," Sasha said.

"He got what he wanted. I should've expected that would

happen with a one-night stand. I told him I wasn't expecting anything serious anyway."

Jasmine grabbed her glass of wine. "To new beginnings and continued friendships."

All of us raised our glasses, toasted to new beginnings, and continued hanging out at the bistro until it was my turn to stay with Lolo Tony at the hospital.

12

BLAKE

"Hey, Maggie. It's Blake Collins. Look, I've been traded to San Francisco and need to sell my house and buy a house in SF ASAP. I'm leaving for the Bay Area late tonight. Call me in the morning and we can work out the details. Thanks." With the sharpness and urgency in my voice, I saw the ride-share driver's eyes staring at me from his rearview mirror as I left the message for my Realtor. I didn't care what the driver thought of me. He needed to mind his business. As soon as the news breaks out that I've been traded, if it hasn't already, I'm sure Dad will be calling me, and that's another issue I have to deal with. Knowing how my dad is, he will probably say that I am a disgrace to the Collins Legacy and that I deserved to be traded. If my mom wasn't there to be the voice of reason and protect me like she had always done, I'm sure he would have disowned me a long time ago.

I arrived at the airport and although I was furious about this trade, I went through security without any issues. My bitter attitude probably would have caused problems, but a couple of the TSA security and airport passengers recognized who I was, even with a hat on, mentioning that they were huge hockey fans. The older generation I met mentioned they were fans of my dad and grandfather when they played with the Crusaders. I took pictures, signed autographs, and talked shop with some of the fans the best I could without the look of disappointment and anger on my face. I just wanted to be alone. Although I didn't want to let my fans down, I already have. I'm going to be wearing a different color jersey and repping a new logo on my chest tomorrow.

After meeting the fans, I went directly to the gate and sat down. There were a lot of passengers at the gate waiting for it to open for boarding. Luckily, I found a small area with no one around. I put on my headphones, then took out my phone and found a playlist to listen to. I brought the bill of my baseball cap down a bit to expand the shadow cast on my face. People needed to take the hint that I don't want to be bothered. Of course, with my luck, someone decided to sit right next to me, but I ignored that person. I didn't even look to see if it was a woman or man sitting next to me, like it mattered anyway. Just as long as this person does not annoy me.

I felt a tap on my shoulder. *What the hell?* I turned to the person sitting next to me and saw a pretty brunette smiling at me. Her dark brown eyes appeared joyful.

"I'm sorry to bother you, but may I use this outlet to plug my phone?" she asked.

"Yeah, sure. Go ahead." I moved out of the way for her to plug her charger into the outlet.

"Thank you."

"Sure thing." I gave a half-smile and took out my phone and started scrolling.

"Not sure if you heard because you had your headphones on but the flight is delayed." *I guess some people can't take the hint.*

"By how long?"

"The agent said possibly an hour or two. Apparently, San Francisco is pretty windy right now."

I sighed. *Now I have to fucking wait here.* "Thanks for the heads-up."

"You're welcome, Blake Collins."

"Excuse me?" I looked at her, surprised that she knew who I was.

"I saw a bunch of people surround you earlier at the terminal and take pictures with you. I asked one of those people who you were, and they said, Blake Collins. I didn't recognize you out of your Crusaders uniform. I know you're a hockey goaltender."

"So, you're a hockey fan?"

"I think it's cool."

Not wanting to be rude to her, I stuck my hand out. "You are correct. I'm Blake. Nice to meet you."

She shook my hand firmly. "Katherine Mendoza. Nice to meet you too."

"So what do you do, Katherine?"

"I'm in journalism. By the way, I know the Crusaders had a game last night. Aren't you supposed to be in New York?"

I guess the news isn't out yet, but I'm not going to tell this woman. She can find out on her own. "I need to take a leave of absence. Not to sound rude, but I would prefer to be alone right now. I'm tired and just don't feel like talking."

"Alright, no problem." Katherine pulled her charger out of the outlet and started to pack up her things.

"Wait, you don't need to leave. I'm just not in the chatty kind of mood."

"Bad day?"

"You could say that."

"I'll just sit here and do some work then." Katherine pulled out a laptop from her bag, opened it up, and started typing.

I glanced to see what was on her screen, hoping she didn't

notice. I wanted to see what kind of journalism she did, but couldn't make out what was on her screen. "Look, I apologize for being rude. I've had a rough day, but I appreciate that you came up to talk to me."

Katherine looked up from her laptop and turned her head toward me. "No worries. Do you want to talk about it?"

"Not really. What kind of writing do you do?"

"I write current events."

"So, you're a news reporter?"

"Yeah, something like that."

"What's your next story about?"

"I'm actually following a lead in San Francisco. I can't really tell you what I'm investigating, but it's sports-related."

Oh shit! Sports-related? I wonder if it has to do with me being traded. Maybe that's why she came up to me when she found out who I was. "Well, good luck with your story."

"Thanks. I'll leave you alone with your thoughts."

AFTER TWO HOURS of waiting at the gate, we were finally able to board the plane. At least the Storm organization took care of their players. They got me a ticket on first class. The two-hour plane ride was pretty smooth until we hit some turbulence approaching San Francisco. The wind coming from the north made it a bumpy ride. *I should have taken some motion-sickness medication.* I gripped on to the armrests, but the turbulence was short-lived. The plane finally landed at the airport.

The Storm organization arranged a car to pick me up and take me to the hotel. They put me up at the Sir Francis Drake in Union Square, which had an old and quirky charm to it. Union Square was a prime area for tourists and shopping. I've visited San Francisco a few times in the past, but I've never really had a chance to explore what the city had to offer. It was almost four o'clock in the morning when I arrived at the hotel and settled in. Being mentally and physically exhausted was an understatement.

Lying down on the bed, I sunk into the softness of the mattress, pillows, and comforter. I turned on the television to ESPN and the two former hockey player correspondents, Devin and Scott, were discussing the highlights of last night's hockey games. I looked at the ticker tape running across the television, and there it was: *CA Crusaders: Blake Collins (#31) traded to SF Storm*. It was probably reported during last night's game when I was seen leaving the ice during pregame skate and I'm sure people probably noticed that I wasn't there and wasn't playing.

One of the ESPN reporters mentioned my name. I turned the volume up on the TV.

"Did you hear that Blake Collins, goalie for the Crusaders, was traded last night to the Storm? It happened during pregame. Take a look at this video," Devin said.

Then I saw myself leaning against the boards talking to Coach Wilson. I was beet red. You can see the fire in my eyes as I glared at the coach.

"Blake didn't take the news well. But that's the name of the game. Players get traded all the time." Scott sounded reassuring as if he knew I was watching the sports update at that very moment, even though it was pre-recorded from earlier last night. "The Collins Legacy on the Crusaders has come to an end."

I blew out a heavy breath of air and grunted in frustration. I haven't spoken to my father yet. I'm surprised. He either didn't know or was waiting for the perfect time to rip me a new asshole. *Fuck!* I needed to get some sleep and stop thinking about this. It's over and done with. I'm with a new team now.

I turned off the lights and left the television on replaying last night's Crusaders game. The screen lit up the darkened room. The sounds of the skates gliding on the ice, players hitting the boards, and fans screaming filled the quietness of the room and the stillness of the night as I dozed off to sleep.

13

ARIANNA

After the weekend of practically living at the hospital, my family and I continued to take turns staying with Lolo Tony in his room. We didn't want him to be alone, and the hospital was gracious enough to let one of us stay overnight with Lolo. They even gave us a pillow and blanket for the chair we sat on. Daddy made sure I wouldn't stay overnight at the hospital on Sunday since I was starting my new job on Monday morning.

I couldn't sleep last night. I was anxious and nervous about meeting the staff of the organization, *my organization*, this morning. I had so many thoughts spinning in my head. *How would they feel about a female owner... a Filipina, for that matter—a minority—leading the organization? What would the team think if and when they find out that I don't know anything about hockey? Will my staff take me seriously?* My restless head led me to get on the internet to search for answers about hockey and hockey organizations. I read about the different hockey franchises and who the owners were. Most certainly, the other owners were not women or Filipino.

I started to panic and regret the decision I'd made. Glenn

was right. I am fucking stupid. He would often call me a 'stupid bitch,' slut, idiot, whatever he was in the mood to say, and that my lounge wouldn't have been successful if Daddy and Lolo didn't help do the work for me. I'm sure Glenn told my grandfather how *he* would manage a hockey franchise if it were *his* team and that Lolo Tony probably told Glenn that the team was practically his because he and I were together and 'practically married.' Glenn didn't own me or my hockey team. That's where they both got it wrong. Glenn would have wanted to see me fail and find a way to take this from me, like everything else in my life.

It was four o'clock in the morning. I had a few more hours until I needed to meet Elliott at Storm headquarters. My nerves subsided a bit, then I dozed off to sleep.

SLEEPING in my old bedroom in my family's home made me feel like I was a teenager again. Flashbacks of Daddy yelling at me and my retaliation of arguing back when I broke the house rules, and then Daddy saying that as long as I lived under his roof, I needed to follow *his* rules. As soon as I graduated from high school and left for college, I never returned to live at home, until now. But this time it was different. When I finished getting ready, I went downstairs to find Daddy cooking breakfast. My mouth watered as I smelled the familiar aromas in the air. He had the coffee brewed as well as what had been my favorite Filipino breakfast growing up: garlic fried rice, over-easy eggs, and pork tocino.

"Good morning, Daddy. Wow! This looks amazing! What's the special occasion that you're cooking food… umm… actually cooking at all?" I laughed then poured a cup of coffee for myself.

Daddy let out a loud laugh. A laugh that I hadn't heard for a long time, since Mama died. Holding the plate of eggs up, he said, "I don't know what you're talking about. I cook... and I think pretty well too."

Giving Daddy a big smile, he did the same. His smile brightened up my morning and this room.

"Arianna, anak. I just wanted to tell you that I'm so happy you're home. It's been a long time since you've been here."

"Me too, Daddy."

After eating breakfast, I left to go to my first day with the San Francisco Storm.

I TOOK a ride-share into the city since I didn't have my car with me. The Storm headquarters was located near the Embarcadero. The driver dropped me off in front of the building, where there was a beautiful view of the bay and Bay Bridge. I walked in the main entrance, pulling one of the tall glass doors open. I was in awe of how much space this building had as I looked around at the simplistic design of the first floor. I walked up to the front desk to find a young woman sitting behind a large computer screen.

"Good morning. How can I help you?" She had a clipped tone to her voice and didn't care to look up from her screen to make eye contact with me. Since it was Monday morning, she probably partied hard over the weekend, and didn't want to be there.

"Good morning, I'm here to see Elliott Reynolds." I stared at her to see if she would glance up, but she stayed glued to the screen.

"Do you have an appointment with him?" Her voice sounded more annoyed as if I was bothering her.

"Yes."

"Can I get your name, so I can let Mr. Reynolds know you're here?"

"It's Arianna Santos." I stared at her, waiting on her reaction.

The young woman sat still for a minute, her eyes opened wide. She slowly looked up from her computer screen. Her face quickly turned a couple shades of pink and she gave an awkward smile to confirm her embarrassment and panicked state simultaneously. By her expression, she realized who I was and stood up from her seated position.

"Oh! Miss Santos. I'm so sorry. Welcome to Storm headquarters. I'll let Mr. Reynolds know you're here. Can I get you anything while you wait?"

"No, I'm fine. Thank you though."

She sat back down and contacted Elliott on the phone to let him know I had arrived. "Mr. Reynolds will be right down." The receptionist stuck her hand out. "I'm Gladys. It's a pleasure to meet you, Miss Santos."

"It's nice to meet you, Gladys." I gave her a firm handshake. "I'll make sure to remember who you are."

Gladys gave a nervous smile.

Then Elliott walked out of the elevator, saving Gladys from feeling even more embarrassed and awkward.

"Good morning, Mi—Arianna. Did you find this place okay?" He extended his arm and we shook hands.

"Good morning, Elliott. I took a Lyft to get here and—"

"A Lyft? If you need a ride next time, please call me. I'll be more than happy to give you a ride."

"That's sweet of you, but I'm fine with taking a Lyft. I don't want to burden anyone. It's only temporary anyway until I can bring my car up here from LA."

"Alright, the offer is open if you need a chauffeur." Elliott smirked and winked.

"Thank you."

"Ready to take a tour of your new home?"

"I'm ready." I looked back at Gladys, who was staring at us, then followed Elliott. *Note to self: Some attitude changes needed to be made starting with the front desk.*

Elliott showed me around and introduced me to my staff. At the end of the tour, he brought me to the tenth floor where my office was located. My office took up the majority of the tenth floor. Walking into the office, the first thing you notice is the floor-to-ceiling windows and the one hundred eighty degree view of San Francisco.

"The view is gorgeous!" I stood by one of the windows near the long wooden desk. My eyes soaked in the picturesque landscape of this city. I was born and raised in San Francisco but I never had the time to actually stop and enjoy it.

"Yes it is."

I turned around and saw Elliott staring at me with a gleam in his bright blue eyes. My palms got sweaty and my face heated up from inside. I was blushing... and flattered. Elliott quickly looked out the window when I caught him staring.

"Umm, is there anything else I should see here?"

"I gave you a tour of the entire place and you met all the staff here, except for the players, coaching staff, and operations staff, which you will meet later this afternoon at our organization meeting."

"Meeting?"

"Yes, I set up a meeting where the whole organization can formally meet you and you can say a few words."

Public speaking?! I started to get a bit flustered and light-headed. I walked toward my desk and leaned on the edge in case I fainted for some reason. I looked at Elliott, who looked concerned.

"Arianna, are you okay? Your face looks a little pale."

"I'll be fine. I wasn't expecting to speak in front of a large group today." I managed to give a slight smile. "I would have preferred to receive advance notice when it comes to meetings, so I have time to prepare, but like I said, I'll be fine."

"I'm sure you'll be great. The organization is not expecting a presidential address or anything like that." Elliott smiled, providing some reassurance to me.

"Thanks, Elliott. If you don't mind, I'd like to explore this place by myself. If you don't hear from me by noon, you can send the troops to look for me. That means I probably got lost somewhere in this building."

He got a good laugh out of that. "I'll definitely send the troops to look for you if we don't hear from you at noon. Have fun exploring. I'll connect with you at noon, boss." Then Elliott walked out of my office.

I sat down, took a deep breath in, exhaled, and absorbed the fact that I *am* the owner of this bad boy. I looked around at my surroundings and I couldn't believe it. *This was mine.*

14

BLAKE

The first practice with the Storm wasn't as bad and awkward as I thought it would be. The guys were cool, including #44 Patrick Greene, who tried to kick the shit out of me when I played against him while on the Crusaders. The team welcomed me as if I had been with the Storm for a while. Coach Chris Hall ran us through drills during practice this morning, which gave me a good taste of the team's style of playing. We continued this practice for a couple hours.

Elliott Reynolds came by at the tail end of practice and waited until we were done to approach me.

"Blake Collins. Welcome to the San Francisco Storm." He stuck out his hand in front of me. "Elliott Reynolds, GM for the Storm."

I gave him a firm handshake. "Thank you, sir. Nice to be here."

"From what I saw on ESPN and the recap of the games over the weekend, you didn't look too pleased to be traded."

"To be honest, sir, I don't think there's anyone that likes to be traded. When you get used to your teammates, it feels like you're leaving your family."

"That's understandable. Well, we are very impressed with your record and feel you will fit right in. We're very lucky to have a Collins' legacy goaltender on the Storm. Have the guys been giving you a hard time?"

"No, sir." I grinned. "You've heard of the Collins Legacy?"

"Good. Yes, I played hockey when your father did. He's an aggressive man."

I laughed. "That's an understatement. At least you're not his son."

Elliott was amused. "Not sure if Coach Hall informed you all but there's a meeting at Storm headquarters at three o'clock. We have a new owner and I would like her to meet the team."

"Yes, Coach told us. I'll be there. A female owner. That's cool."

"I think she'll do an awesome job with the organization."

"That's great. I'll finish up here and get ready. See you at headquarters, sir."

GOING BACK to the hotel to drop off my gear before heading out to Storm Headquarters, my Realtor called me. I was getting worried when I didn't hear from her yesterday.

"Hey, Maggie. Thanks for getting back to me."

"Of course, Blake. Are you sure that you don't want to keep your house here in LA?"

"Yeah, I don't know when I'll be back in LA or if I'll ever want to stay there permanently."

"Alright, I'll put up a listing soon. I'll refer you to a friend in the Bay Area to help you find a place in San Francisco. Her name is Sloan Murphy. She'll take care of you."

"Thanks, Maggie. Let me know if there are any offers. I plan to go to LA to grab more things within the next week depending on my schedule."

"I'll keep you posted. Take care."

"Bye."

Soon after, my phone rang. Thinking it was Maggie again. I answered the call without checking the caller ID.

"Hey, Maggie, was there something else you needed to talk to me about?"

"Yes, like when you were going to tell me that you were traded." A deep, gruff voice sounded from the other line. *Fuck! It's Dad.*

"Hey, Dad. Sorry, I thought you were my Realtor."

"What the hell, Blake? You got traded to the San Francisco Storm?! You realize that team has lost a majority of their games so far, and will probably not even qualify for playoffs?"

"Dad, it's still early in the season. I'm sure with me being part of the team, things will change."

"You think *you* can turn this team around? It's not like you've been playing your best either, Blake. You haven't been the same since your knee injury. No wonder the Crusaders traded you."

"I've accepted that I'm with the Storm now. There's nothing I can do. Players get traded all the time. You need to accept it too."

"You're a Collins and are supposed to stay with the Crusaders. Plus, I heard that the new owner of the Storm is a woman. I'm sure she will cause the organization to tank. Hockey is a *men's* sport."

"Seriously?! It is what it is, Dad. I haven't even met the new owner yet. I'm pretty sure she has a plan to make the franchise great. Why else would she own a hockey team?"

"When did you get so weak? Are you partying or in a relationship? You *need* to focus on hockey. No exceptions."

"I am focused. I'm not partying and not in a relationship."

"Good."

My father wasn't sensitive to feelings and didn't care how I felt. All that mattered was his reputation and how I represented the Collins' name.

WHEN I ARRIVED at the San Francisco Storm building, the first thing I admired was the aesthetics. The building had a modern feel to it and it didn't seem overly decorated. Entering the building, I saw some of the teammates huddled to the side.

"Hey, Blake. Over here, man," the Storm's captain, Brandon Owens, yelled out and gestured for me to go over where they were.

I walked over to Brandon and the three other teammates that were with him.

"We're about to head upstairs to the second floor where the meeting is being held. First time here?"

"Yeah, Cap. It's a cool building. I'll follow you guys. I'm not sure where everything is."

"All good, Blake."

We crammed into the elevator and headed to the second-floor auditorium. It was a short, smooth ride to the second level. One of the guys said that Storm employees could watch away games here on the big screen. Walking into the auditorium, some of the guys on the team were already seated and motioned to the seats around them that were reserved for the team. This room was fucking awesome. It was like a movie theater with stadium seating, a large screen for viewing events through the projector, and a stage in front. All that was missing was popcorn and alcohol, but I'm sure they provided that, I just didn't know where it was.

I sat down with the rest of the team, greeting each other with a bro hug. Being with this team started to feel as though I had known them and played on the team for a while... and it had only been a few hours since officially meeting and practicing with the guys. We sat near the stage. Close enough to see the speaker's face as well as the speaker being able to see our reactions.

The room quickly filled up with the corporate execs from the upper floors. Elliott walked in with a confident stride toward the stage. He stopped by the team to chat with a couple of the guys, Coach Hall, and the assistant coaches. Elliott and I made eye contact, and he nodded his head. I relayed the greeting back to him in the same way. Then he went on stage.

"Hey, everyone, please find your seats. We'll be getting started soon."

The echoes of all the chatter quieted down and people were taking their seats.

Elliott proceeded. "Good afternoon, ladies and gentlemen. Thanks for coming to the meeting. I'm sure you've probably heard that there were a few changes to the organization within the last few days. Many of you met her earlier today when I gave her a tour of corporate. I would like to introduce the new owner of the San Francisco Storm franchise who is also the granddaughter of Antonio Santos, Sr.... Miss Arianna Santos."

It was *her* that walked onto the stage. *Oh shit!* My eyes grew wide. I couldn't believe it. Out of all the fucking places in the world that we could run into each other. She was the *same* Arianna that I saw naked. The same woman that I kissed all over her body, who made passionate sounds when I pushed deeper in her tight, wet pussy, and the one that led me to believe she was single. I hope she couldn't see me.

I heard a couple of the teammates whisper comments that Arianna was "hot for a curvy Asian woman," "this organization was going to tank," and "why the hell would she buy the franchise?" *If they only knew how I know her.* I quickly changed the expression on my face. I didn't want anyone on the team to suspect that I knew Arianna... especially intimately.

"Thank you, Mr. Reynolds. Hello everyone. Like Elliott mentioned, my name is Arianna Santos, and I am the new owner of this franchise. As some of you know, my grandfather, Antonio Santos, Sr., or best known as Tony to most, is in the hospital after suffering a major stroke. As he rehabilitates, and we all hope for his speedy recovery, I have accepted the position and responsibility as the owner of this franchise. It's my pleasure to support this organization to the best of my ability. I appreciate the hard work you all have done, and I look forward to seeing this franchise become the next Stanley Cup Champion."

A loud roar from the crowd and applause echoed through the auditorium. She definitely knew what to say to make the crowd hyped. I watched her body language, and she was different from when I met her at Blue Velvet Lounge. She couldn't stand still. She was fidgeting with the notecards she held and read from. Her voice was trembling. Arianna was nervous.

"Thank you, Miss Santos," Elliott said as Arianna stepped aside for Elliott to take over the microphone and podium. "Part of the plan to get to the playoffs and finals is to have a solid team." *What the hell is he going to do? Please don't call me up on stage.* "I would like to introduce you to the newest player and goaltender of the San Francisco Storm, Blake Collins." *Fuck!* "Come on stage, Blake." *Now Arianna was definitely going to notice that I was here.*

I stood up and made my way toward the side of the stage where the stairs were. Arianna and Elliott were facing me as I slowly walked up each step. The light from above the stage didn't illuminate the side, I was barely able to see where my foot was landing. I looked at Elliott and then Arianna. As soon as the light shined on my face, Arianna's expression changed. She did her best to smile, but her eyes were wide and in shock. I gave Elliott a firm handshake but when I grasped Arianna's hand to give it a shake, an electric charge hit every nerve in my body, awakening all my senses... and my cock. With the way she was gazing into my eyes, I'm pretty sure she felt it too.

From the corner of my eye, I noticed Elliott staring at both Arianna and I. "Nice to meet you, Miss Santos." I let go of her hand and just stood next to her, facing the audience under the hot lights from above the stage. I can feel this energy between us that I haven't felt with any other woman. I didn't want the whole organization to see the bulge in my pants, so I tried to think of something to calm it down. I remembered the picture I saw of Arianna and her man in her office. That definitely softened up my manhood.

Elliott went back to the podium. "Blake Collins came to us from the California Crusaders. We're lucky to have this skilled individual on our team. Like Miss Santos mentioned, the Storm is ready to become this year's Stanley Cup Champion. Let's continue to support our team. Keep fighting, gentlemen."

The auditorium filled with cheering and applause once more. From the sound of the crowd, this franchise was ready for all the changes and for something good to happen. Elliott concluded the meeting shortly after. I was moving quickly to get off the stage to avoid any awkward interaction with Arianna, but then Elliott stopped me before I could even place my foot on the first step.

"Blake, hold on a minute," Elliott said as he gestured for Arianna to move closer to him.

"Sure, sir."

"You may not be aware, but Arianna is pretty new to the world of hockey. I think it would be a good idea if you two spent some time together, so she can learn more about the game."

"With all due respect, sir, why are you asking me? Why not Coach or the captain?"

"Well, I thought about it and since your family is a legacy on the ice, you have a lot of expertise in the sport. You live and breathe hockey. Also, since you both are new to the Storm franchise, it would be good to bounce ideas to Arianna from your experience with the Crusaders."

I glanced at Arianna then back at Elliott. "Yes, sir. Sounds good unless Miss Santos prefers to work with someone else."

Arianna gazed at me then smiled and looked at Elliott. "Working with Mr. Collins would be fine, Elliott. That's a great idea. Thank you."

"My pleasure, Arianna. I'll leave you two to discuss business," Elliott said as he walked off the stage.

"Thanks, Mr. Reynolds," I stated.

Arianna and I were the only people left in the auditorium. There was an awkward silence between us. She barely looked at me when Elliott left. Her head was turned away, looking toward the empty seats of the auditorium. *I might as well break the ice.*

"So, are we going to discuss the elephant in the room?"

15

ARIANNA

What the fuck, bro? If Blake really wanted to go there, then we'd go there.

"You want to discuss what happened between us a couple weeks ago? We should go to my office for privacy. I don't want to talk about my personal life here." I snapped at him.

"Fine. I'll follow you." Blake waited for me to walk off stage, then walked behind me like he was my bodyguard.

We entered an empty elevator car. I used my key card and pressed the button for the top floor. When the doors closed in front of us, Blake turned and cornered me in the back of the elevator. He brought his arms up and pressed his palms against the wooden interior behind me. His palms by my ears, caging me in. My back pressed against the wooden panel. Tensing up, my eyes shift around the elevator, making for an escape plan. I had no flash of insight into what he wanted to do to me.

"Do you know how hard it's been trying to forget you and that night at your lounge?" Blake moved his face closer to mine. I can feel the warmth of his breath on my skin.

"It—"

Ding. Saved by the bell. We reached the tenth floor and Blake quickly released his hold before the doors opened.

I stepped out of the elevator car and Blake followed suit. We went inside my office and I shut the door behind me.

I turned around to face Blake, glaring at him with fire in my eyes. "Let me tell you something, Blake Collins," I said sternly. I wanted his attention. How dare he try to intimidate me in the elevator. "I was so hurt that you didn't even say goodbye that night. I know I said that I wasn't looking for anything serious but that night was so amazing. I replay everything that we did in my office... all the time. Don't think you're the only one trying to forget it. I thought that maybe now that I'm not in LA, I'd be able to forget about you. Yet here *you* are. What are the freakin' odds?"

Blake stared at me without a word. He had a serious expression on his face. His eyes were laser-focused on mine. "Are you done?"

"Excuse me?" Forcing myself not to blink, I wasn't backing down from his stare. My eyes seared into his. "Yes, I'm done."

"You lied to me."

"What the hell are you talking about?"

"You told me that you were single. Yet I saw a picture of you with another man on your bookcase. You could have at least hid it somewhere to appear single before you took me into your office. I also agreed that I wasn't looking for anything serious, but sleeping with someone who is married or in a relationship is not my thing. It's nonnegotiable. That's where I draw the line."

Oh my God! My eyes widened. *That's why Blake left.* "I didn't realize—"

Interrupting me mid-sentence, Blake said, "That night was a spur-of-the-moment thing anyway. I knew it would be a one-time thing, so I left and didn't look back... and like you said, what were the odds of us meeting again?"

"I get it now. Why you left the way you did. I'm sorry, Blake. I didn't lead you on though. I was single then and am single now. To be honest, I forgot I had that picture on my bookcase. That guy in the picture was my ex-boyfriend, and he left me for someone else," I said, not disclosing to him that Glenn broke up with me the same day we had sex.

Blake's expression softened up a little, looking more relieved after hearing me out.

"Blake, would you like to sit down?" I smiled and motioned to the chairs in front of my desk, remembering we were in a similar set-up in a different office.

"Sure, Miss Santos."

"Please, call me Arianna. Why do you have to be so formal?" I laughed as I sat behind my desk.

"You *are* my boss now. You own me." Blake smirked.

"Let's get the facts straight, Mr. Collins. I own the team. I don't own *you*." I smiled back at him, lightening up the mood in the room. "However, *you* can claim me anytime," I said in my sexiest voice. I winked.

Blake's cheeks turned pink and his eyes darkened. I remembered that same look he gave me before I let him possess me that night at Blue Velvet Lounge... the same look he gave me in the elevator just a few minutes ago.

Looking at him was triggering flashbacks of what we did intimately together and it was making my panties damp.

"We need to handle some business. Mr. Reynold's gave me an assignment to complete with you. I guess you can call me your hockey teacher." Blake winked and gave a mischievous grin.

"I'll do my best to listen and take notes, but I've been known to get easily distracted, so I may need a lot more hands-on learning to keep me focused." It was so easy to flirt and tease Blake.

"I think that can be easily arranged."

"So Mr. Collins, what do you want to teach me first?"

"Actually, do you want to go grab an early dinner, and then we can get started with the lessons?"

"That sounds good."

"I don't know the area well, but if there's something you're craving or want to go to, let's go. I'm open to anything."

"I think I have an idea of where we could go eat. There's a place I've been wanting to try. But before we go, can I ask you something?"

"Of course, Arianna."

"Is this considered a date? Now that I'm the owner of the Storm, dating within the organization doesn't look good."

"No, it's a business meeting to discuss hockey," Blake said with a serious tone in his voice.

"Okay cool." *Well, not really.* I was hoping he would say that he wanted it to be a date and that this would be risky. He now knows that I'm single, but I guess going out to dinner with Blake for a business meeting is better than having dinner alone tonight. "Let me pack up my things, and then we can be on our way."

WE ARRIVED at the Fillmore area to this quaint Asian fusion restaurant called Royal Ginger Bistro. I've read great things about this restaurant on social media, and that the lines can get pretty long, so an early dinner may give us the advantage of a shorter wait time for a table. After fifteen minutes, we were escorted to a small table toward the back of the restaurant.

Blake pulled the chair out for me. I was surprised. I sat down with my mouth pretty much agape, he noticed it when he sat down in front of me.

"What? I do have manners, you know. My mother taught me how to properly treat a woman... especially a gorgeous woman."

His voice sounded very sincere. His hazel eyes sparkled with flecks of gold from the flickering flame of the candle sitting on the table.

"Your mother taught you well." I smiled, then looked at the menu. "I'm paying, by the way. It's on the organization since this is a business meeting, and not a date." I glanced up quickly to catch his reaction.

"I guess I can't argue with that, or with my boss for that matter." Blake chuckled while looking down at the menu.

I grinned. "Let's order first, then we can discuss hockey. So what do you want to try?"

"This Royal General Chicken sounds good, but I'm open to anything."

Shortly after being seated, we ordered our family-style entrees for us to share as well as a couple alcoholic drinks. We delayed the discussion about work until the waiter left.

"Can I ask you something, Arianna?"

"Of course."

"If you don't really know anything about hockey, why did you purchase the Storm franchise?"

"Well, it was given to me. My grandfather bought the franchise as a gift for me for my birthday. Apparently, his name and mine are on the agreement. Since he had a major stroke and is in the hospital, I decided to step up and take over. I wasn't planning to be involved much since I don't really follow sports."

"Oh. I'm sorry to hear about your grandfather."

"Lolo Tony is doing rehab so hopefully, he'll be able to make a full recovery."

"Lolo?"

"Yes, in Filipino, that's how we address our grandfathers."

"So you're Filipino? That's why you're beautiful and exotic looking. I would have guessed something completely different if you were to ask me what I thought your nationality was. Plus your last name threw me off." He had a sly smile like he was thinking something naughty.

I blushed, trying to find a way to hide it. *Blake called me beautiful and exotic.* I'm flattered. Then I laughed. He was about to get schooled on Philippine history. "The Philippines were claimed by Spain and was a Spanish colony for over three hundred years. That's why the Filipino language consists of Spanish-sounding words. I don't want to dull you on the history of the Philippines, but that's pretty much the gist of it. By the way, Philippine women are referred to as Filip*ina*."

"Thanks for my history lesson of the day. I learned something new."

Our drinks arrived. We clinked our glasses together, then took a sip.

"So Mr. Collins, it's your turn to teach me a lesson for today. What will my first lesson of hockey be?"

"Well, aren't you an eager student?"

"I'm excited to learn. I want to get an A-plus."

The corners of Blake's mouth curled up into a sexy smile, and it's taking me a lot of willpower not to touch him, grab him, and kiss him. *I'm his boss.* I need to ingrain that in my head.

Blake took another sip of his drink. Then said, "Have you watched a hockey game before? Either live or on TV?"

"Nope. I already told you that I don't really follow any sports. All I know is that hockey is played on the ice. There are players that need to use that stick thing to hit the puck thing into their goal."

Blake nodded his head up and down. He looked down at his hands that were around his drink. He didn't make eye contact with me, but from the way his mouth was pursed, it looked like he wanted to laugh. "Okay, okay. Glad to hear that you know the concept of the game."

"What? I can tell that you wanted to laugh." I rolled my eyes and took a swig of my fruity cocktail. "So we're all good or is there more I need to learn?"

"I apologize. What you said sounded so cute." He smiled and let out a laugh. "But there's plenty more to learn about the sport. Looks like our food's coming so why don't we take a break and get back to it later."

"Okay, that sounds like a plan. My stomach is growling anyway. I can't think on an empty tummy."

"After we finish up here, I want to take you to a place for hands-on learning. I think you'll be able to grasp the concepts easier. It'll be fun."

"You won't tell me where we're going?"

"I think it will be a nice surprise for you." Blake grinned.

A surprise? "Okay, I'll go along with the teacher's plan."

Our waiter brought our meals to the table. It smelled as amazing as it looked.

"Bon appétit!" the waiter said as he placed the last entree we ordered on our table.

Blake and I smiled and thanked our waiter, then began to eat our meal. During dinner, I caught Blake glancing at me, and when I noticed his eyes on me, he quickly looked away. It was cute. There was such a boyish charm to this sexy man. I wondered what else there was about him that would make me fall for him more... I had to remind myself though that *I was his boss.*

16

BLAKE

"Great choice for dinner, Arianna," I said as we both got into a ride-share vehicle. We were on our way to the surprise location that I insisted we go to to get more hands-on hockey training. I was actually hoping to take her to my hotel room, but I let that thought quickly slip out of my mind.

"Well, you can thank social media. Royal Ginger Bistro had great reviews. They actually lived up to the hype. I give it five stars." Arianna raised her hand with her palm and five fingers faced me.

I gave her a high-five, which made Arianna smile from ear to ear. I thought her smile was the cutest. It made her more youthful-looking and you can tell that she was genuinely happy. "I agree. Food is five stars. Service is five stars. Great company is also five stars."

"You're not so bad yourself, Blake. I had a great time considering this was a business dinner."

"Remember, we're not done yet. I have one more place to teach you about hockey."

"I'm nervous but also kind of excited."

"You'll be fine. We're almost there."

As the driver approached close to the Bay View Ice Center, I turned my head to look at Arianna. She was looking out the window and up at the tall buildings that covered the narrow and busy streets of San Francisco's financial district. With the sun setting, the orange glow of the sun peeked between the buildings and radiated onto Arianna's golden skin. She looked absolutely gorgeous.

"Arianna, we're almost here."

"Where are we?" Arianna's voice was shaky and her eyes looked worried.

"You'll soon see." I smiled in hopes to provide Arianna some reassurance. "You don't have to worry about anything. I'll make sure you're safe."

She smiled back. "Thanks, Blake."

My hand on my lap, Arianna took hold of it, giving a gentle squeeze. That sent a bolt of electricity throughout my body. Besides the quick high-five earlier, this is the first time today that I've had any physical contact with her where the touch seemed to linger on my skin when she let go. I'm doing my best not to cross the line, although I just wanted to pull her closer to me and give her a deep, long kiss. I wanted her hands running through my hair, and to feel her tongue in my mouth.

Suddenly, the driver stopped the car in front of the Bay View Ice Center, the Storm's practice rink. Not only did the vehicle stop, so did the inappropriate thoughts I had of my new boss. I needed to remember to keep this professional, no matter how much I wanted her. *She's my boss.*

"Hold on, Arianna." I got out of the car and walked around to the other side, opening the door for her. "I am a gentleman, remember?"

"Wow! I am really impressed." She smirked.

"You are upper management, and I need to make a great impression for my first day on the job." I extended my hand to help her out of the vehicle.

Arianna giggled as she took hold of my hand. "Why, thank you, Mr. Collins."

"My pleasure, ma'am."

"If I were you, that would be the first and last time you say ma'am to me." She glared at me and was not the happy self she was a second ago.

"I'm sorry, Miss Santos." I looked down in embarrassment.

"I'm only half kidding." Arianna smiled again. "But I really don't like being called 'ma'am.' It makes me feel so old."

"I won't say that again... I promise." I closed the car door after Arianna stood next to me. Then we walked side by side toward the main entrance of the ice center, and I punched a code to unlock the doors.

"So where are we?"

"We're at the Bay View Ice Center. This is where the team... *your team* practices." I pulled open the main entrance door and Arianna stepped inside. "Follow me."

I took Arianna into the practice area and showed her around. Although I've only been here once, I had time to check this place out after team practice earlier today in order to familiarize myself with it.

"Are we the only ones here?" she asked.

"I believe so. The rink closes at six o'clock, but I asked Elliott if there was a way I can use it today to help you learn about hockey. And he gave me an access code."

"If I knew we were going into the rink, I would have brought a coat, and maybe some pants. Wearing a dress is not ideal." Arianna shivered and she looked uncomfortable. I should have thought about this thoroughly before trying to surprise her. I didn't know why I wanted to surprise her in the first place. It's not like I was allowed to date her anyway… and who knew if she wanted me. *She was my boss now, and she made that clear earlier.*

"I think I have something you can cover yourself up with." Entering the side door leading into the players' locker room, I went to my locker to retrieve my duffel bag. Unzipping it to open it wide, I shuffled through the bag. I pulled out my practice jersey and handed it to her. The equipment manager gave me a few jerseys, and since today was my first practice, I had a couple clean, unworn ones. "Here, try this on."

"Are you sure? Don't you need to use it to play in?"

"They gave me a few, so this one hasn't been used yet. I don't want you to be cold."

Arianna pulled the jersey over her head and it was loose on her but still hugged some of her voluptuous curves. It looked good on her.

"How do I look?"

"Sex—it looks good on you."

One of Arianna's eyebrows lifted up. I almost said *sexy*. But I wouldn't be lying. Arianna was wearing *my* jersey, and she looked so damn sexy in it. Her dress was nowhere to be seen underneath the jersey. It looked like she was wearing only the jersey and her high heels. I would love to see her only wearing my jersey and her heels, naked underneath the Storm uniform, waiting for me to come home from a game. *She's your boss. Get that in your head, Blake! Not your other head!*

"Thank you. What are you going to teach me now, Mr. Collins?"

"Let's go back to the rink. We'll get you some skates." I grabbed my skates and threw them onto my shoulder and took some hockey sticks and a puck as well.

"Wait. Ice skates?"

"Yes. That's what hockey players use when they're on the ice."

"I know that. I just... well... don't know how to ice skate." Arianna blushed in embarrassment.

"Oh. It's all good. This can be part of learning about hockey too. It will be fun."

We headed back into the practice rink. I got her a pair of skates in her size and knelt down to lace them up for her.

"Thanks, Blake." I looked up at her as I finished lacing the second skate. She was watching me. Her dark brown eyes darkened as my hand accidentally brushed against her calf. That look was everything. I recognized it from our one and only night together.

I stood up, extended my hand, and she took hold of it as I assisted her off the bench. "Are you ready to get on the ice?"

"I think so." Arianna glanced down to the ice.

"Don't worry. I got you."

Arianna nodded in agreement that she was ready to learn how to ice skate. I held both her hands, facing her, while slowly bringing her into the rink. The crunch of the metal as our skates touched the icy floor echoed in the large room.

"Arianna, how are you feeling?"

"I'm okay, I guess."

"Alright then, you're going to slowly move your legs so you can glide forward. I'll still hold your hands, but I won't be pulling you this time."

"I'm scared."

"I got you." I made eye contact with her the whole time. She gripped my hands tighter, I knew I was her safety net on the ice.

"Okay." Arianna started moving her legs slowly. She was wobbling and a bit unsteady as she should be since it was her first time skating.

"Keep your eyes on me. You're doing great."

Arianna's smile was as wobbly as her legs. Her eyes couldn't focus on mine. They were shifty and she started to freak-out. Her breathing shallowed and quickened. Arianna was losing her balance and unable to gain any control. I pulled her close to me and wrapped my arms around the small of her back.

"I got you like I said I would. Take a deep breath and try to calm down for me, okay?" I slowed us down to a complete halt. We were in the middle of the rink.

Arianna's breathing slowed down back to normal. Her hands were clutching tightly to my shoulders. Her eyes stared back at mine. I never let my gaze lose the connection with hers.

"Thank you, Blake," she said in a gentle whisper.

"I would *never* let anything happen to you." The volume of my voice matching hers. "You're my boss and I need a paycheck." I laughed.

Arianna laughed out loud and slapped my bicep. That made her lose her balance again, but I pulled her in tighter to keep her steady. She gasped.

"Speaking of being your boss. I know that I said we need to keep this professional because I am the boss of this franchise, but can I tell you something?"

"Of course…"

"I so want to kiss you right now. There was just something about you when we met at the lounge, I couldn't get over you. I never thought I would see you again."

My gaze became more intense after hearing that. That electric current I felt earlier came back in full force, surging through my veins as we stood so close to one another. "Well…" I wrapped my arms tighter around her waist. "I feel the same. Don't get me wrong. I was fucking angry when I saw you today. All I kept seeing in my head was the picture of you and your ex-boyfriend in your office."

Arianna looked down. I pressed my forehead against hers, continuing to keep my line of vision on her eyes.

"But when you explained everything, I was relieved. I'm also trying to be as professional as I can be since I know you're my boss... but all I kept thinking about was being close to you and wanting to press my lips against yours."

Her eyes looked back up, staring into mine. I pulled my forehead away from hers. *Fuck it.* I leaned down and planted a deep kiss on her soft, full lips. Arianna kissed me back. I've been craving her lips and her touch ever since we met. Tightening my hold around her waist, I pulled her in closer. She let out a soft moan as our tongues twisted and tangled around one another's. Arianna lifted up her arms and placed her hands behind my head, her fingers tousling my light brown mane.

With our kisses becoming more intense, the sensual sounds Arianna made became more frequent. My pants suddenly felt a bit tighter below my waist. I held her so tight that I'm sure that she felt my length as it grew hard. I knew that we couldn't take this any further than this kiss. I needed to listen to my brain, not the lust I felt from my other head. After a couple minutes, I pulled my lips away from hers. Standing there in the middle of the ice rink staring at each other, smiling from ear to ear.

"Umm... so that just happened," I said, feeling surprised yet somewhat satisfied.

"Yeah, it did..." Arianna was still playing with my hair. "...but I liked it."

I couldn't stop gawking at her.

"What?" she said reluctantly.

"You're so beautiful."

Arianna's cheeks turned pink, and she looked away shyly. "You're so sweet. But I don't think I'm that beautiful."

I cupped her face with my hands. "I don't know what you're talking about. You're gorgeous."

"Thanks, Blake."

"I'll always remind you that you're beautiful because you are."

As I admired her beauty, Arianna's expression told me that

she had something on her mind. "I really like being this close with you, but can you *please* get me off the ice and teach me about hockey on the bleachers or something?"

"You really don't like this?" I laughed.

"Not the ice part."

"You're cute."

"I thought I was beautiful." Arianna gave a sly smile.

"Miss Santos, you're amazing, beautiful, gorgeous, cute... I can go on."

Arianna's smile was contagious. I couldn't help but smile back at her.

"Thank you, handsome, for making me smile... now get me off the ice! That's an order from your boss."

"Alright, alright."

WE STAYED at the rink for a couple hours. I taught Arianna about the playing area, equipment, teams, and penalties... all from the bench. Her eyes started to glaze over, and she wasn't really engaging as much with her questions and comments. I knew she was done for the evening. After the kiss, I held back any physical contact with Arianna. I needed to focus on the task that Elliott gave me to do. I didn't want to give him any indication that I couldn't fulfill the task of teaching Arianna about hockey.

"Miss Santos, I think that's enough hockey talk for the night."

She stared at me, unsure if she fully processed what I just said. She looked like a deer in the headlights. "Huh? Can you repeat that again, please?"

"Exactly. It's time to call it a night. You look exhausted."

"I'm fine. I can talk about hockey all night."

"Really now? Then what was the last thing I just explained?"

She paused again. Her eyes were looking elsewhere as she tried to recall the last topic I had explained to her. "How hockey is fun?"

I laughed out loud. "Umm, not quite. I was talking about the penalty box and power plays."

"Okay, you're right. It's been a long day and I'm tired. Plus, I need to wake up early, so I can visit Lolo Tony at the hospital before I head to the office."

"Let's pack up and I can call a Lyft or cab for you."

"So you're not leaving yet?"

"I am. I'll set up my own ride too. Why do you ask?"

"I'm just wondering. I thought we would be sharing a ride again. That's all." There was a hint of disappointment in Arianna's voice.

"Actually, it may be best to share a ride. I want to make sure the boss gets home safely."

"Blake, it's alright. I'm a big girl now."

"No, I insist."

"I would rather not. My father is at home, and I don't want him to see me with anyone from work. Even though I am an adult, he still waits up for me. It's kind of sweet if you think about it. I hope you understand."

"I do. That's really cute. You're a daddy's girl. Has he always been like that?"

She giggled. "I'm more like Daddy's princess." Arianna sweetly smiled. "Daddy wasn't always like that. When I was younger, after my mom passed away, it seemed like he wanted to be in control of my life and needed to know where I was…. All. The. Time. I rebelled a lot. We argued often, and I was never home. As soon as I was eighteen, I packed up to go away to college in LA and never came home unless it was for our monthly family dinners that started a year ago."

"A rebel? I can kind of see you as one." I winked at Arianna. I loved that she gets easily shy and bashful when she gets a compliment or when I looked at her a certain way.

"If you insist on having me ride with you, I can drop you off first to where you're staying then I'll head home."

"Alright, that's fine." I was happy that we still got to spend a little more time with one another. "I'm ready. Let's go."

17

BLAKE

"Blake, I didn't get to ask you if you were a mama's boy." Arianna angled her head to look at me while we were in the back seat of the Lyft car.

"I am. My mom has been my number one supporter since I could remember."

"How about your father? If you don't mind me asking, is he still around?"

"I don't mind. He's still with my mom, and I don't really get along too well with him. He just loves me because I followed his footsteps with hockey." I moved my head to peek outside the car window.

"Don't say that. I'm sure he loves you for more than just being in hockey."

"Well, it doesn't seem that way."

"My mama and I butted heads a lot when I was growing up, but we got closer before she passed away."

I turned my head back to look at Arianna, by then she had looked outside from her window. "I'm so sorry. I didn't—"

"It's been over ten years since she passed away. No need to feel sorry for me." Arianna snapped.

In a low voice, trying to reassure her, I said, "It's still the loss of your mom, even if it's been a while, I'm sure it still hurts knowing she's not here." The closest I had to losing someone close is my grandfather. I couldn't imagine what would happen to lose a parent at a young age.

"Thank you, Blake. I appreciate it," she said softly. Arianna didn't look back in my direction.

I reached out and held her hand. She squeezed it. I figured it was a sign that she appreciated the company. The rest of the car ride was silent, and Arianna's gaze remained toward her side of the car, out the window. I just remained quiet and gave Arianna her space.

We arrived at the Sir Francis Drake Hotel.

"Well... we're here. This is where I'm staying." I opened the car door.

Arianna let go of my hand. I leaned in to say goodbye and the light from inside the car illuminated her face. It was glistening from tears that flowed down her face. I pulled her toward me and held her. Her head was against my chest.

"Let's go inside, and we can talk in private."

Arianna nodded her head. "Okay," she whispered.

WE ARRIVED at my hotel room, one of my arms was still wrapped around her back and holding her waist. I held the door open and gestured for her to go ahead. I followed behind her into the room and closed the door behind me.

"Arianna, would you like anything to drink?"

She spun around facing me, eyes red and puffy from crying. Then the sexy, buxom woman stepped forward and wrapped her arms around my waist tightly. She fit perfectly into my body as I enveloped her in my arms, tightening the embrace.

"I'm sorry for crying. This is so embarrassing." Her voice soft and raspy.

"No need to be sorry. Did I do something to make you cry?"

"No, I was just thinking about my mom... then Lolo Tony in the hospital." Arianna sniffled. "I've been so overwhelmed with everything."

"I hope you know that I'm here for you." I didn't know what else to say. My chin rested on top of her head, and I just stroked her luscious hair to help her relax. I wanted to be there for her as a friend even if we were not allowed to be anything more.

"Thank you." She said, muffled against my chest.

We sat down on the bed and talked more about our lives growing up, our families, all the expectations they had for us, and what we wanted for the future. I did my best for that hour not to touch her. I had her on my bed and all I could think about was doing more to her on said bed.

"Are you feeling better?"

"Yes, now that I'm here with you." She smiled, her eyes sparkled.

"I'm glad. I had a good time hanging out with you..." I sighed.

"What is it, Blake?" Her eyes searched for something in mine.

"Nothing. I think I should get you home soon. I know you need to wake up early to go to the hospital to visit your grandpa."

"Oh." She stood up from the bed. "Okay, that's fine. I'll ask the concierge to help me call a cab." She barely looked at me. "Thanks for everything, Blake." Arianna veered quickly toward the door.

I raced behind her. "Wait, Arianna."

She latched on to the doorknob and opened the door slightly, but I managed to stretch my arm out and I pushed it closed with the palm of my hand.

"What are you doing? I thought you wanted me to go." Arianna still held on to the doorknob and turned it once more.

I slipped in front of Arianna, staring closely at her beautiful face as my back leaned against the wooden door. "I just said I think I should get you home soon. I didn't say you had to leave right this minute."

Arianna had a confused look on her face.

"... I... don't want you to leave." I barely knew Arianna, but I didn't want to let her go.

The curvaceous, tanned vixen let go of the metal lever and instead locked the latch above it. "I don't want to leave either. I want to stay with you."

"I thought you had rules, Miss Santos. You couldn't be with anyone in the organization."

"I'm the owner, Mr. Collins. I could break those rules as long as no one finds out."

"Well then. This will be our little secret."

"Good." Arianna had a mischievous smile. Her eyes pleading and filled with desire.

I wanted to be the one to fulfill that need and desire. I wanted to give her everything she craved. Licking my top lip, my eyes scanned up and down her body slowly.

Arianna placed her hands on my chest and pushed me with a force that caught me off guard. She pinned me against the door, clenching my shirt. Her face moved in, then her lips changed course aiming toward my ear instead of my lips. Her cheeks brushed against mine, sending a bolt of energy down my body with her touch.

"Give me one of your Storm jerseys, handsome. I want to be comfortable," she whispered in a sexy voice, then nipped my earlobe with her teeth.

With my eyes closed, that pinch sent shivers down my spine. "Handsome?" I said softly in her ear, smiling.

Arianna's teeth released my earlobe. "Yes, because you are

definitely handsome, Blakey." Feeling the shift in her stance, I opened my eyes, watching her back away from me. I immediately caught hold of her waist before she could flee away from me again.

"Where do you think you're going, beautiful?"

"I want your jersey, so I can get comfortable. Did you think I was leaving again?"

"Maybe." My hands traveled down the curve of her hourglass waist to her round ass.

Arianna reached and held on to my hands, removing them off her plump buttocks before I could squeeze those cheeks. "Uh-uh. Not until I get your jersey."

I smirked. "Alright, I'll get it for you, beautiful. You're very persistent."

"I know what I want." She smiled and winked.

In my closet, I scoured through the apparel that hung neatly on the rack. I pulled my new team jersey off the hanger and handed it to Arianna. "Are you pleased with this one?"

"Perfect." She accepted the oversized black jersey with the Storm logo and my last name and number on the back. She clutched the piece of clothing in her hands and brought it up to her nose, smelling it.

"I haven't worn it yet if you were hoping it had a particular scent on it."

"I'll be right back." Arianna raced to the bathroom.

After a few minutes, she peeked her head out the bathroom door. I sat on the edge of the bed waiting for her.

"Ready for a fashion show?"

"I'm always ready for you, beautiful."

My eyes went wide and my jaw dropped when she came out of the bathroom in what looked like only the jersey and her high heels. *She must have read my mind from earlier this evening at the practice rink.* Her hair cascaded down her back, and she'd applied a dark red lipstick to her luscious, full lips. She looked so sexy wearing *my* jersey. Just like earlier today when she wore my practice jersey while on the ice. This one draped over her body loosely but accentuated the curves of her waist and hips. Her legs were tanned, and I noticed a flower tattoo near her ankle.

"That look on your face says it all. I guess you like this." She motioned her arm up and down her outfit as if she was modeling a prize on a game show.

Arianna was my prize for being part of her hockey team. "I'm speechless. You are one gorgeous woman. My jersey looks amazing on you."

"Good." Arianna strutted toward me, her high heels showing how toned her calves were. She stopped before me, leaning forward and cupping my face with her soft hands.

Placing my hands over hers, I took in the warmth of her hands against my skin.

Closing the distance between us, she lifted one leg at a time, bending her knee and placing it on the bed respectively, straddling my hips. The jersey lifted up as she sat on my thighs, exposing her ass and a black satin thong. Placing her lips on mine, she applied a slow, delicate kiss.

My hands trailed down from her face to the curves of her waist. I reached around her plump ass, squeezed her cheeks, and then traced the edge of her panties with my fingers. She grazed her teeth on my bottom lip then gave it a suck. Her hands lowered and clutched on to my shirt and lifted it over my head and off my body. I reached for the jersey, but she tapped my hands.

"No, handsome... tonight I will call the shots."

My eyes darkened with greed and desire as she emphasized her need to control this.

She caressed my chest, following the grooves of my abs and muscles with her fingers, then she pushed me suddenly onto the bed. Still straddling my groin, her sex sat right on top of the bulge protruding from my jeans. My bulge pulsated on the area between her legs.

She got off me and stood by the edge of the bed. Arianna leaned forward, grabbed hold of my leather belt and unbuckled it. Soon after, my jeans were unbuttoned and unzipped.

"Mmmm," Arianna hummed and bit her bottom lip as she pulled my pants and boxers off my legs. "I think I've waited patiently enough, wouldn't you agree, handsome?" Her voice low and sexy.

"Yes, I completely agree."

She got on the bed and knelt by my hip, facing my erection. My cock hard and with a slight curve to it. Arianna licked her lips. She stroked the hot and hard flesh between her fingers, then leaned down. Her tongue exploring the entire shaft starting from the swollen head to the base, then sucked on my balls. She licked her way up to the tip of my cock, then her lips encircled my throbbing erection. She lowered her head, taking my steely length deeper in her mouth.

I inhaled sharply. Her head bobbed up and down savoring my length. It felt fucking good. I groaned as she went down again, taking it farther into her throat. "Fuuuck!"

Arianna got up before I could reach my peak, then straddled my groin, my rigid flesh against the satin of her panties. She pulled my jersey off her luscious body, exposing her bare chest. Her tits, perky and waiting for me to devour. She got up on her knees, pushed the black satin fabric to the side, and took my cock in her tight opening.

She let out a whimper. "You feel so fucking good." Her hands placed on top of my chest.

My heartbeat and breathing quickened. I growled at the feeling of the tight walls of her pussy surrounding my engorged length as she slid up and down slowly and steadily. I touched her swollen clit underneath the satin cloth with my fingers and rubbed. She arched her back, her hands moved behind her and gripped my thighs. Arianna was grinding faster as I rubbed her sex rougher. Her moans got louder. She clenched as she reached her peak.

"Ohhh!" Her body shuddered as she burst with pleasure all over my cock.

The lust and desire on her face were enough to send me over the edge as well. I groaned as I held her waist and thrust upward. Pounding harder and faster until I reached the brink. "I'm coming," I said, breathy and low. A wave of pleasure traveled through my body as I released my hot cream inside her.

Arianna leaned forward and placed a gentle kiss on my lips. She was glowing. I smiled at her, gazing into her dark brown eyes as I placed a loose strand of her hair behind her ear. Cupping her face, I admired everything about her.

She got up and off me, grabbing my jersey, she threw it onto the bed. Arianna laid down next to me and handed me my jersey.

"When you wear this during your games, I hope you think of me." She snuggled closer to me.

I brought the jersey up to my nose and inhaled. Her sweet scent was all over it.

"I don't think I could ever get enough of you, Arianna. I have craved your touch, kiss, and body since the day we met." I told her as we laid in bed, holding each other, legs intertwined and her head on my chest. I kissed the top of it and she tightened her embrace.

"Blake, you're all I've thought about since literally running into you at the lounge. I have you now and don't want this to end."

"Stay." I lightly caressed the smooth contours of her back with my fingers.

"I wish I could, but I should get home soon. I texted my dad while I was getting ready in the bathroom earlier and told him that I was going out with friends. I don't want him to worry."

"I understand. I want to make sure you get home safe. So call me when you're in the car on your way home and stay with me on the phone until you get inside your house."

"Yes, boss." Arianna sat up on the bed. "There's a problem with that… you never gave me your number." She giggled.

"Well, that's an easy fix. Where's your phone?"

"It's in my purse." She pointed at the desk by the window.

I got up from bed and went to the desk. I grabbed her purse and handed it to her.

Arianna took out her phone from her satchel and handed it to me. "Number please?" she said in a cute, high-pitched voice.

I stood by the bed next to her, added my contact information, and saved it on her phone. Then passed it back to her. "Here you go."

Arianna looked down at her phone and smiled. "Handsome? I like that."

I winked at her. "I was thinking of putting 'Sexiest Man on Earth' but that didn't seem appropriate… yet."

Arianna laughed and rolled her eyes. Her thumbs were typing something on her phone.

I tried to look over her shoulder to see, but she brought the phone up closer to her chest, so I wouldn't be able to make out what she was typing out. I did have a chance to glance at her plump and perky breasts that were situated next to her phone. I bit my lower lip. *Damn!*

She smirked and looked up at me. "Are you liking what you're seeing?"

"What?" I was caught off guard by the alert notification from my phone. I picked it up from the side table and noticed a text message from Arianna:

Hi, handsome. Now you have my number. Expect to get more than just texts from me. Xo, beautiful P.S. Maybe I will send a picture of my girls since you're admiring them as I type.

I saved her contact information as *Beautiful* on my phone, and showed it to Arianna proudly. Her eyes sparkled in the light from my screen. "I can't wait to see what these 'more than just texts' are." I grinned. Just thinking about what I hoped she would text me had my manhood stiffening up.

Arianna saw it growing and her eyes darkened with desire. "I think your friend wants to come out and play again."

18

ARIANNA

"I'm inside now. I'll talk to you later. Goodnight," I whispered on the phone talking to Blake. It's two o'clock in the morning, and I really hoped not to wake up Daddy. The kitchen light was shining through the darkness in the living room. I peeked through the doorway of the kitchen and Daddy was sitting there alone, a tan-colored drink in hand. Probably his usual scotch.

"Hi, Daddy. Hope you weren't waiting up for me."

His gaze turned to me as soon as I spoke. "Hi, anak. No, I couldn't sleep."

"Are you thinking about Mama?"

"Yes, but also everything going on with your Lolo Tony and now you're an owner of a hockey team. I'm getting stressed."

"Why are you stressed about me owning a hockey team, Daddy? Do you think I'm going to fail?" I walked into the kitchen and sat next to him at the breakfast bar.

"No, anak. I'm worried how others will react toward you—a confident Filipino woman—in a predominantly male sport." My father's eyes shifted back to his glass. "I don't want to see you get hurt."

"I've grown up and can take care of myself. Don't worry, Daddy." I gave him a kiss on his cheek. "I'll spend time learning about hockey and the organization. I won't let you, Lolo Tony, or my franchise down. You'll see."

"Okay, Ari. It's getting late. Hope you had fun with your friend tonight."

"I did. We had a great time catching up." *Oh I did alright... with my handsome Blake.* "You go to bed soon. Goodnight, Daddy."

"Goodnight, anak."

***

STRETCHING my arms out from underneath my cozy blanket, I woke up early this morning with a huge smile on my face. I was surprised I even slept. Getting less than five hours of sleep will usually have me dreading getting out of bed, but last night was incredible and I couldn't wipe this grin off my face. It had been a while since I've felt this way. I reflected back on last night's encounter with Blake and felt so giddy, like finding out when your middle school crush liked you back or scoring floor seats to your favorite boy band's concert so you can see *NSYNC up close and personal. Grabbing one of my fluffy pillows, I covered my mouth and shrieked into it.

Since it was only seven in the morning, I'm sure Daddy was still sleeping. He was still in the kitchen after I wished him 'good night.' Before I got out of bed, I reached for my phone charging on the nightstand and sent a text to Blake.

Good morning, handsome. Hope you slept well. I didn't sleep much, but it's all good. Hoping to see you later today. XO

I got out of bed and combed through my clothes to figure out what outfit I should wear today. After taking a quick shower, I changed into a white long-sleeved button-down blouse and black pants, then hastily put my makeup on and put my hair up into a ponytail. Grabbing all of my belongings for work, I went downstairs and found Daddy done with cooking breakfast and Kuya Eric sitting at the breakfast bar. My eyes widened with surprise to see both of them in the kitchen before seven-thirty a.m. The smell of the garlic fried rice, fried eggs, and bacon had my mouth watering.

"Good morning, Daddy. I'm surprised you're up cooking. Did you sleep at all?... Good morning to you too, Kuya. It's pretty early for you to be up."

"Good morning, anak. Kain na tayo. I cooked breakfast for us. Let's eat together before you go to work."

"Sure Daddy. I still want to visit Lolo Tony before I go to headquarters."

"Morning, Ari. How was your first day on the job yesterday?" Kuya Eric asked.

"It wasn't that bad. I'm trying to learn about hockey quickly. I still have a lot of research to do."

"That's cool. I heard the Storm had a trade over the weekend and you have a new goalie—Blake Collins—from the Crusaders. Heard he is a hothead and that he could get suspended from the league if he keeps that up. Not to mention, he's a total player and womanizer. Better watch out for that guy if you run into him." My brother mentioned.

You got to be shitting me? Is Kuya Eric's news legit? My brows furrowed and I looked away thinking about Blake. "Where did you get all that information from?"

"ESPN and TMZ."

"Oh my God, Kuya. TMZ? Really?"

"What? They're reliable."

"Anyway, I met the team briefly yesterday at our staff meeting. I met Blake too. He doesn't seem that bad."

"Alright, Ari. I'm just watching out for you."

"I'll do my research and if I need to know any gossip news,

I'll be sure to ask you first." I started laughing. Daddy was laughing as well.

"Daddy, may I use one of the cars today to get around the city?"

"Of course, anak. The keys are hanging by the garage door."

"Thanks, Daddy."

I kept quiet through most of breakfast. I kept thinking about what Kuya Eric said about Blake. *Is it true?* Should I be worried about him? My thoughts were interrupted with a text alert from none other than *Handsome.*

Good morning, beautiful. Sorry for responding late. I just woke up. I didn't sleep well. All I thought about was you. I'm meeting with my Realtor today to try to get a condo. Let's meet later this evening. x

I put my phone back down on the kitchen counter.

"Is everything okay, anak?" my dad asked me.

"Yes, Daddy. I need to get going. Thanks for breakfast and for letting me use your car." I got up and gave him a kiss on the cheek, then picked up my things.

"Bye, anak. Drive safely."

"Bye, Ari," Kuya Eric said and gave me a fist bump on my way out.

On my way to the garage, I passed a mirror hanging on the wall, and gave myself one last look hoping I didn't go out looking like a hot mess. I pulled out my mauve-colored lip lacquer from my bag and touched up my lipstick. Puckering my lips together, I then flashed a smile. *Alrighty, I'm ready!*

ON MY WAY to the hospital, I stopped by Starbucks to get my usual and something decaf for Lolo Tony. I thought he would appreciate something from the outside other than what the hospital was serving him. I'd ask the nurse to thicken up the liquid so he wouldn't choke swallowing it. Lolo was moved out of the intensive care unit and into a regular hospital room yesterday. The doctors felt he was stable enough and had improved.

Before going up to the floor where Lolo was at, I decided to reply to Blake's text. After typing and erasing a couple of times while trying to figure out what to tell him, I finally sent the text.

I'll be in the office in a bit. I'm still at the hospital visiting my grandpa. I'll check my schedule and let you know if I can meet up with you later this afternoon. Hope the condo works out! Xo

I sighed, putting my phone back in my purse, then traveled to the fifth floor. As I entered the hospital wing where Lolo's room was located, I checked in at the nurses' station. Lolo Tony's nurse thickened the coffee for me before I visited Lolo, and gave me his new room number.

I walked around the long hallway. *Where is room 30A?* I followed the signs and eventually made it to his room. Approaching closer to the doorway, I heard a familiar voice. I stopped and listened quietly, trying to figure out who was visiting him this early on a Tuesday morning.

"I know, sir. Arianna is a special woman and I hope she finds someone to love and make her happy," the man said.

Oh my fucking God! My eyes opened up wide. I stormed through the doorway.

"Oh hell no! What the fuck are you doing here, Glenn?!"

My outburst blindsided both men. Glenn stopped talking. My grandfather stared at me with a look of disappointment.

"I'm sorry, Lolo. I didn't mean to startle you." I smiled at him. "Good morning, how are you?" I glared at Glenn, then walked farther into the room.

Lolo's speech was delayed and it took him time to find his words. "Good... morning... anak," he slurred. Moving to the other side of the bed, I leaned over to give my grandfather a kiss on his forehead. I also did not want to be next to Glenn.

"I got you a surprise." I extended my hand to show Lolo a white coffee cup with the infamous green Starbucks logo. "The nurse had to thicken it, but it's something different from the usual drinks you get here."

The corner on one side of his mouth lifted up, giving me a slanted smile that was most sincere. I grabbed his hand and gave it a small squeeze.

"Lolo, if it's okay with you, may I speak with Glenn alone?"

Lolo nodded that he approved.

With a blatant look at Glenn, I walked toward the entryway. Passing by Glenn, I slowed down next to him and coldly said, "Meet me outside in the hallway."

I couldn't make out what Glenn was saying, but I heard the sound of his voice faintly behind me, then footsteps. I waited in the hallway for a brief moment, then Glenn walked out of the room. He had his jacket in one hand and stood facing me, expressionless.

"So, what did you want to talk about?" He had a snarky tone to his words.

With my arms crossed, I glared at him for a moment. My brows furrowed, lips pressed into a thin line, eyes seared into his soul. "Why the fuck are you here?" I kept my voice low, not wanting to draw attention to us from the hospital staff, visitors, or other patients.

"In case you didn't notice, I was here to visit Lolo Tony when you so rudely interrupted."

"Excuse me? He's *not* your Lolo. He's mine. You are no longer part of this family. *You* made that clear a few weeks ago when you decided to leave me for someone else."

"I've known Lolo for as long as we were together and developed a bond with him… he's like another grandfather to m—"

"Oh bullshit," I interrupted him. "Tell me the *real* reason you're here. You probably heard that I'm the new San Francisco Storm owner, right... and you probably wanted to take it from me?" I was serious. My gaze fixed on him with beady eyes. "You came to visit Lolo Tony to convince him to transfer the ownership to you, am I right?"

Glenn's face turned red. He was getting angry the more I called him out. He didn't have anything to say. He just stared.

"Well, it's too late Glenn. I'm the owner now. This franchise will stay in *my* family. I don't want to see you here again or anywhere near me or my family."

"What the hell, Ari? I guess our breakup really got you going crazy. I understand. You're angry and want to get back together again?"

"Hell no! You wish. I'm happy you left me. It made me realize how much of a jerk you really are. You controlled and manipulated me while we were together."

Glenn's eyes widened and his mouth opened slightly. He was surprised and looked around the hallway.

I kept going. "I accepted it because I thought that was normal in relationships. I was blinded by it because I thought you really loved me. All you did was use me and take advantage of my family. I will say it again. I don't want to see your ugly ass face near me or my family." I blazed past him and headed back toward Lolo's room.

I HOPED my visit with Lolo Tony would have been a little longer, but I really needed to get to work. It was my first week as the new Storm owner, and I'm still learning all about hockey and the franchise. I also wanted to do some research about Blake, especially after the comment Kuya Eric made earlier.

I arrived at headquarters and went straight to my office. Only greeting the front desk receptionist and the security guard as it seemed no one else was around. Walking into my office on the top floor, I stood by the window and peered at the view outside. I just couldn't get enough of the view of the San Francisco Bay. It was so gorgeous. I still couldn't believe this was mine.

I sat down on the large executive chair behind my desk, peering around at *my* office. I didn't get a chance to go through my desk yesterday. Rummaging through each drawer, I noticed a remote with four buttons. There wasn't a television anywhere I could see, so I pressed the buttons to see what they did. *Oh shit!* One button frosted the windows in a couple seconds, another unfrosted them with the same speed, the third button turned on the lights, and the last button turned them off. This was way too cool to be my office, and obviously my predecessor, before Lolo bought the team, wanted his privacy. These functions, especially the privacy windows, were a very special touch to this office.

Enough messing around. I needed to get to work. I took my laptop out from my work bag, powered it on, and was ready to rock. I couldn't wait to research Blake. It had been on my mind for the last couple hours. *Damn you, Kuya!* I guess it didn't hurt to check it out. Blake and I didn't know each other too well. It's been a couple weeks since he and I met. I shouldn't completely trust Blake, but oddly I do.

I went onto Google and searched *Blake Collins California Crusaders*. A whole slew of images and articles about him popped up. *Blake Collins: Golden Child for the Crusaders, Collins Legacy Lives On,* and *NHL Sexiest Players 2018* were among the top articles for him. I found an interesting article from a Hollywood insider that Blake was a womanizer. There were pictures of him with different women, who were all beautiful and looked like models. We did live in Los Angeles. Women that lived in Beverly Hills and Hollywood had money, came from money, or found a way to be with someone with money.

Looking closer at the photographs, Blake was captured on camera with women coming out of restaurants, bars, the nightlife in LA. The ladies were completely opposite of how I looked. They were tall, leggy, blondes or brunettes... and one thing was certain, none of them were of a minority race. I think I'm going to be sick. My tummy felt like there were tiny, little people making knots with my insides and playing tug-o-war with it. *Kuya Eric was right.* Blake looked happy with these women. They were *his* type.

What the hell did he see in me? I must be just another fuck to him. I'm nobody special to him, just another side piece he could get while he was here in San Francisco. I was glad to find this out about him now before I became too invested in him emotionally. I'm not looking for another guy to play games and take advantage of me. I'm better than that.

19

BLAKE

"Good morning, Mr. Collins. This is Sloan Murphy. I'll meet you at the condo after lunch and see what you think of it."

"Sounds good, Sloan. I will see you at one o'clock as scheduled. Maggie told me that there may be some potential buyers for my home in LA, so hopefully, I like this property and these transactions happen seamlessly and simultaneously."

I hung up and looked at my phone, hoping to see three little dots next to Arianna's name letting me know she was texting me back. I knew she was visiting her grandfather at the hospital this morning and was probably busy. I wanted to text her again, but I won't. It might make me look desperate, but I wanted to see her later today, so I'll just wait to text her later. After last night, I hoped she felt the same. I would love to see her smile, hear her sexy voice, feel her silky skin, savor her voluptuous body, and indulge in her scent. Every. Damn. Day.

I made a mental note that I needed to get my car from LA later this week or at the very least, get a lease on a new car, so I didn't have to rely on ride-share transportation anymore. The chaos of the trade and seeing Arianna again made me realize my life in LA was now in the past, and I needed to start building my future as part of the San Francisco Storm franchise and settle down here in the Bay Area... hopefully having a future with Arianna.

I threw my practice gear into my duffel bag, leaving early for practice so I could get some alone time in the rink. *My sanctuary.* Before leaving for practice, my cell phone rang. Hoping it was Arianna, I grabbed my phone out of my pocket and saw the caller's name on the screen. *Dad.* Of course it was. I took a deep breath in and forcefully let it out. I mentally prepared for whatever my dad wanted to talk to me about.

"Hello."

"Blake."

"Hey, Dad. What's up?"

"Well, I think you need to up your game. You've been playing horribly since your return from being injured. Now that you're on another team, I think you need to step it up to show the Crusaders that they made a mistake so they will buy you back. The Crusaders *will* get you back."

Listening to my dad got me irritated. "So what does that mean? I was actually leaving for practice to get an early start and *work* on my game." I said sharply.

"Blake, watch your tone. I'm just trying to help you—"

I cut him off before he pissed me off even more. "Dad, I appreciate your help, but the trade is done. You need to understand that I'm with the Storm now. I'm moving forward and will work with the goalie coach on my game." I calmly told him.

"That's not enough. I have hired a private goaltender trainer. He will be meeting you later this afternoon."

"I'm looking at a condo later this afternoon, so I can finally settle in."

"I'll ask to have him meet you after practice tomorrow then. He'll work with you then."

"What's his name?"

"I'm not sure. It was a recommendation from Elliott Reynolds. Mr. Reynolds and I spoke yesterday and thought it would be best to hire a private trainer to work with you aside from team trainings. I'll call your general manager and ask him to reschedule your meeting until tomorrow."

"That's fine. Thanks, Dad."

"I'll check in with you tomorrow after you work with the trainer."

Then in typical Drew Collins fashion, my dad did not reciprocate the thanks I gave him, and he just hung up without saying goodbye. Rolling my eyes, I put my phone back in my pocket. *My dad was such a jerk.*

PRACTICE WAS DEFINITELY BETTER than it was yesterday morning. Today had been my second time practicing with the team, and I'm getting better acquainted and adjusting to their style of playing fairly quickly. The sounds of skates on the ice, the hockey sticks slapping the puck, and my teammates yelling out during a play is what I lived for. What would complete this moment would be if Arianna watched the game and there was a crowd cheering.

Dad's words repeated in my head. 'You need to up your game.' I need to prove that I don't need a private trainer. Coach Hall noticed my skills today and seemed pretty impressed.

"Alright Blake. Nice save. Stay aggressive."

I nodded back at Coach, acknowledging and appreciating the feedback.

I've started to really like being part of this team, even more so now that Arianna was here too. It didn't matter that she was the owner of the franchise, I just wanted to be with her. Team practice lasted for a couple hours as we prepared for a game we had in a few days. It was my first game playing as a Storm, not to mention, my first home game with the team. I hoped to make my team proud... especially the owner.

Needing to meet the Realtor at the condo listing in an hour, I raced to the locker room to get ready. After showering, I searched through my duffel bag and took out a clean gray polo shirt, dark denim skinny jeans, and my Calvin Klein boxers. I picked up my phone to check the time and noticed a text from Arianna. She mentioned that she needed to look at her calendar. I hoped that she was available to see me later. I knew that we should be careful when hanging out. There was a huge risk to my career as well as hers if we got caught. She was worth the risk though.

"So, Mr. Collins, what do you think of this property?" Sloan Murphy, the tall, busty blonde real estate agent, asked me.

"It's great! I want to make an offer. Please, Mr. Collins is my father. You can call me Blake."

"Perfect, Blake. Let me get the paperwork ready and I'll call to make an offer to the homeowners." Sloan blushed and grinned.

"Please let them know it's a cash offer. So hopefully we can negotiate a fair price for this place."

"Yes, will do. Please excuse me as I get the paperwork completed."

I nodded to acknowledge Sloan's statement.

The condo was in the North Beach area of the city. The views from the balcony were breathtaking. I could see the Golden Gate Bridge, Bay Bridge, Pier 39, and Alcatraz in the distance. I stood on the balcony soaking everything in. It was like a photograph on a postcard, telling your family and friends 'wish you were here.' All that was missing was my *Beautiful* standing by my side. I took my phone out of my pocket and took a picture of the view, and texted Arianna to show her how amazing it was. I finally felt like my life was getting better and better each day.

Hey, beautiful. Look at this view from the condo. I'm making an offer and hope the seller will consider it. Are you free to meet up later? I want to see you.

I walked around my future home and noticed all the modern finishes of the place. Stainless steel appliances, marble kitchen countertops, kitchen island, farmhouse sink, recess lighting in the living room, dark gray hardwood floors, lots of cabinets and closet space, and an open floor plan. This condo is much more homey and intimate than my home in Los Angeles.

My Southern California home was a large two-story home with five bedrooms, three bathrooms, large kitchen, family room, living room, swimming pool, patio with fire pit and wet bar in the back yard, long driveway, and a four-car garage. I converted the four extra bedrooms. One bedroom was turned into a home gym, two bedrooms were guest rooms for my parents and sister when they visited, and the last room became an office. From what Maggie told me when she showed me that property, it was formerly owned by a 1940s Hollywood movie star, who had passed away and his children sold the home. The home was very nice, but way too big for only one person living there. It was lonely.

Sloan returned with a huge smile on her face.

"Great news, Blake. The seller was able to lower the asking price since we gave them an all-cash offer."

"That is great news."

"With that said, the seller accepted your offer and you are now the owner of this lovely home. Congratulations, Blake."

"Sloan, that is fantastic news! Thanks for your help finding this place." I walked up to Sloan to give her a high-five, but she moved in to give me a hug instead. I stood there with her arms wrapped around my shoulders and her big boobs pressed against my chest. My arms remained to my side. This was awkward.

"You're welcome." Sloan backed off, still smiling. "This calls for a celebration. Let's go out to dinner and celebrate tonight."

"That sounds fun, but I have plans tonight."

Sloan looked away. "No worries. I thought it would be fun to hang out and celebrate this sale."

A text notification sounded from my phone. I pulled my phone out and I smiled. There was a message from Arianna.

Hey, you. I won't be able to meet later. I have some things to take care of at the office and wanted to spend time with my family. Hope you understand.

My smile faded. Even though it was a text, I felt like she may be upset with me. I sent her a text right away.

That's alright. I totally understand. Have fun with your family.

"Well, Sloan. My plans just changed. I'm free to hang out tonight. Let's celebrate my new home."

20

BLAKE

S loan and I went to the Little Italy area of the city, and to a quaint Italian restaurant by St. Peter and Paul Catholic Church and Washington Square Park. There weren't many patrons inside eating when we arrived, so we were seated right away. There were black and white portraits of famous landmarks of Italy hanging on the wall and the vibe was very rustic like we were dining in Italy's countryside. This restaurant was family-owned and the staff had been exceptional so far.

We got seated at a table next to a window. There were four chairs and I pulled a chair out for Sloan then took my seat across from her, which was next to the window.

"I think I would prefer my view from this side. Would you mind if I sat next to you?" Sloan asked as she sat down on the chair next to me.

"Umm… sure, I guess."

"What do you think of this restaurant?"

"It's cool."

The waitress came up to our table and asked for our drink order.

Sloan turned to me with a big grin on her face and excitement in her eyes. "How about we get a bottle of champagne?"

"I didn't plan to drink since I have practice tomorrow morning, so I'll just take an ice water with lemon." I crossed my arms on the table, looking down at the menu.

"Okay, sure. I'll take a glass of your house Cabernet please."

The waitress wrote down our drinks, then informed us she would be back with them and to take our order.

As soon as the waitress left, Sloan turned to face me once again. She placed her hand on my forearm. "Blake, how long have you been playing hockey?"

I uncrossed my arms and shifted in my chair, moving away from her. Her hand dropped to the table, and she pulled it back to herself.

"I've been playing since I was a kid. So how long have you been in real estate?"

"About five years."

"Cool. That's nice that you take your clients out to dinner when you close a sale."

"I actually have never done it before. You're my first one." She moved her chair closer to me. From where the chair and table were positioned, I was cornered against the window. She placed her hand on my knee. *Whoa! What is Sloan doing?* "I think you're very handsome and Maggie told me you were single. I was wondering—"

My forehead beaded with drops of sweat and my heart was beating quickly. "You know, Sloan, you're really nice and I appreciate your help with the house, but I am not looking to date anyone right now. Plus, I'm your client—"

"As soon as the house closes, you won't be my client anymore." She smirked. Her hand still on my knee.

"Yeah, I'm flattered, but I'm not interested in dating anyone. I think it would be cool to hang out as friends, but nothing more. I hope you underst—"

My words were cut off by the ringing of my cell phone. It was sitting facedown on the table. Picking it up and looking at the caller ID, it read *Beautiful*.

By the look on Sloan's face as well as her hand lifting from my knee, she had read the caller ID too.

"Can you please excuse me while I take this important call?"

Sloan nodded and faced away from me.

Looking out the window, I answered the call.

"Hey, beautiful," I said softly.

"Hi, handsome." Hearing Arianna's voice was soothing to my soul. "What are you doing?"

"I'm out to dinner."

"Oh, I was going to see if you wanted to have dinner, but you're already out."

"How about we go out for dessert?"

"Oh I know what I want for dessert." The way she said dessert, it sounded so sexy that I knew what she wanted.

"You're probably thinking the same thing I am."

The waitress returned with our drinks and asked us for our order.

Sloan told the waitress what she would like to eat, and I pointed at what I wanted to order from the menu in front of me.

The phone fell silent.

"Hello? Are you still there?" I asked, then looked at my phone screen to see if Arianna was still on the line.

"I'm still here... umm... who's having dinner with you? I heard a woman's voice."

"It's my real estate agent, Sloan Murphy. She wanted to celebrate since I got the condo."

"Oh, she did? Does she do that with all her clients?"

"Umm—"

"That says it all. She just wants to sleep with you, Blake," Arianna snapped.

"No, she doesn't. Can I meet you after dinner, please?"

"Fine. Let me know when you're done with dinner. I'll just stay here at the office and meet you somewhere." Her voice went from sexy to monotone so quickly. Arianna was irked.

"Okay beautiful, I'll call you when I'm done here."

"Bye." Then she hung up without giving me a chance to say goodbye.

Great. Arianna was upset with me.

I let out a sigh as I placed my phone on the table.

Sloan took a sip of her wine. Turning back toward me, she asked, "Everything okay?"

"Yeah, it's good."

"Girlfriend issues?"

"You could say that. Look, Sloan, thank you again for helping me find my new home and wanting to celebrate it, but I have to go." I grabbed my phone and stood up.

"I understand. No worries. Go handle what you need to do." Sloan stood up at the same time I did and gave me a hug good-bye. I didn't hug her back. My arms were hovering over her back then I patted it lightly, needing to move past her to leave the table. As Sloan released her embrace, she moved in quickly and planted a kiss on my lips.

I pushed her away. "What the fuck, Sloan?"

"I thought that you should get a taste of what I can provide you."

"What the hell for?"

"It sounded like you were having issues with your *beautiful*, so I wanted to remind you that I'll be here if things don't work out."

"Sloan, things between you and me will *never* work out. I don't feel anything for you. I'm sorry if you thought different... I really need to go. Excuse me."

Sloan stepped aside and remained silent as I moved around her.

When I finally got outside of the restaurant, I was about to call Arianna, but then I saw a text message from her.

Obviously, you're busy with another hookup. I decided to just go home. Good night.

Arianna was overreacting and I needed to talk to her. I called her a couple times, but it went straight to voicemail. *Ugh.* I decided to just go back to the hotel. Tonight didn't end as I hoped it would, but maybe if Arianna and I spent tonight apart and slept on it, we would be able to hash things out in the morning. I texted her back.

There's nothing going on between Sloan and me. I left in the middle of dinner hoping to see you, but you texted that you went home. Let's please talk about this tomorrow. Good night.

I HAD trouble sleeping last night, maybe I got a good three hours of sleep. My mind was restless. I played back what had happened during dinner last night and my conversation with Arianna over and over again. Now that I'm up early, I got dressed to go to the rink. I wanted to get some 'me time' before hockey practice and meeting my private goalie trainer, which was just a waste of Dad's money, but if Elliott and Dad felt I needed this, then I'd go with whatever they wanted. I didn't have a choice anyway.

I arrived at the practice rink with an hour of alone time. I skated around, ran some drills, and stretched before the rest of the team arrived. Team practice had the same vibe as yesterday. The team practiced well this morning and I felt my skills were adapting to how my teammates played. When practice ended, I stayed on the ice.

Besides me, Brandon was the only other person left in the

rink as everyone else went back to the locker room to shower and go home.

"Hey, Blake, you did good today. Aren't you going to get ready with the rest of the guys?"

"Thanks, Cap. I'm waiting for the private goalie trainer my dad hired. He wants me to up my game."

"That's serious, bro. Well, good luck. I'll see you at practice tomorrow."

"Alright Cap. See you tomorrow." I went to the bench to wait for my new trainer.

A few minutes later a tall, slender guy with dark brown hair and tanned skin briskly walked through the double doors of the rink. As he got closer, I stood up and noticed that he looked vaguely familiar. He soon stood in front of me at eye level.

He stuck his long arm out. "Blake Collins, I'm your new goaltender trainer. The name's Glenn Ayala." He had a strong, low tone to his voice.

I took off my glove and gave him a firm handshake. "Nice to meet you." I was trying to remember where I'd seen this guy. His name sounded familiar too.

"Is everything okay?"

"You look familiar. Have we met before?"

"We've met before. Back in Canada."

"Really? When?"

"Grade school. St. John Paul Elementary School. Does that bring up any memories?"

You've got to be *kidding me?* My eyes opened up wide. The only Glenn I remembered was a bully that made my childhood hell. I stared at him, trying to picture the younger version of him.

I clenched my jaw and fists. A flood of memories surged through my mind and body. "I do remember," I grunted. "You made my childhood a living hell. I hated going to school because of you."

"Hey man, that was a long time ago. I was young and stupid. Can we move past that?"

"Yeah, I guess." I still resented everything he put me through in elementary school. He tormented me, telling me that I wasn't good enough, a failure, and that my family didn't want me... nobody did.

"Alright, great. Let's get started."

Glenn had me running drills and watched my form with the puck as he slapped some toward the goal.

"Blake, keep your glove up!"

I am, dammit! I followed what I was told to do.

"I said keep your glove up!"

I brought up my glove once more, trying to remain calm.

"Goddammit, Blake, I told you to keep your goddamn glove UP!"

That was it. I threw my stick down. *Clack.* The sound of wood hitting the ice echoed in the rink. I pulled my gloves off and threw them down next to my stick, and skated quickly toward the face-off circle where Glenn was shooting pucks. My face turned red from the rage I felt inside. I finally reached where he was standing. I was about an inch away from the point of his nose. Whatever he was thinking of doing to me, I was not going to put up with it... not like when we were kids.

"What the fuck is your problem, Glenn?" I snarled. My arm lifting up, seconds away from punching his fucking face.

"I told you three times to keep your glove up, but you're refusing to listen."

"The hell! I put my glove up every time you yelled out."

"Your father was right. I spoke with him this morning, and he mentioned that you don't listen."

"What's your problem, man?"

"I don't have a problem, Blake. Obviously, you still do."

"This is not going to work." I skated away and grabbed my hockey stick and gloves from the icy floor.

Glenn just stood there. "Look, Blake. Elliott and your father told me that you needed this training to get better. You just need to listen. That's your problem..." he yelled out as I skated off the ice.

Fuck off! I gave him the bird and left him hanging on his words and alone on the ice as I pounded the pavement to the locker room. I will not be bullied and humiliated by him again.

21

ARIANNA

I woke up to Blake's text from last night. I don't know what came over me. *Why was I even jealous?* Blake and I weren't even exclusive or dating. We weren't supposed to be anyway. I should be upset with him though. He's a player and a womanizer. He knew I was busy last night, but he went out anyway with the next woman that was accessible to him, and it happened to be his real estate agent that he was with earlier that day.

Argh. With all that happened yesterday, I couldn't help but feel upset. First, seeing Glenn visiting Lolo Tony pissed me off. Second, learning about Blake's dating history. Then, actually experiencing Blake being with another woman at dinner that same day. What the hell? This clearly was a sign that Blake and I should not be together.

I scrolled through my text messages and sent a text to the group chat I had with my girlfriends.

Good morning, ladies! What's new? I think I have bad luck with the guys I'm attracted to. Let's go to happy hour soon. I need it! Xo

I got up from bed, went through my luggage, and picked out

an outfit for today. I'd packed fairly light, expecting to return to LA within a week, but that may not happen. I needed to go back down to SoCal to get more clothes and bring my car up. I also needed to check on Blue Velvet Lounge. With all that had been going on, I forgot to do my daily follow-up yesterday with Britney. I have cameras around the lounge and checked on the staff twice since I've been here in San Francisco. I sent a text to Britney.

Good morning, Brit! Just checking in on how it's going with BVL. Hope the staff isn't giving you a difficult time. If they do, let them know that I'm watching them on the cameras. LOL. I may be visiting this weekend. I'll let you know. Call me if you have any problems. Miss you all. You're doing great, boo!

I placed my phone in my bag and decided to finally go and take a shower and worry less about everything on my plate at the moment. After my steamy hot shower, I got dressed in black high-waisted skinny pants, black tank top, and dark gray tunic cardigan. I wore my wedge booties. I love the fall weather. It's my favorite time of year.

I told Daddy yesterday that I wasn't planning to have breakfast at home so he didn't have to cook so much food. I thought of stopping by Starbucks to get a Pumpkin Spice Latte and something to eat. Grabbing my work bag and purse, I heard my phone ring a few times alerting me of incoming text messages.

Lorelei, Sasha, and Jasmine were texting that they were down to hang out for happy hour, but needed to check their schedules. Britney responded, letting me know that everything was fine at the lounge and the staff had been pretty responsible and respectful to her. The tone of another text notification alerted me. This time it was from Blake.

Good morning, beautiful. I want and need to see you. Can we please meet today so we can talk? Xo

I stopped what I was doing, taking a couple of deep breaths to clear my head before I responded to him.

Hey, you. I can meet you at Starbucks this morning at eight o'clock. It's the one near your hotel. Let me know if that works for you. Thanks.

I didn't want to express any affection or endearing nick-names to him. I didn't want to lead him on, especially if I was just another booty call. I got in my daddy's car and was en route to Starbucks, hoping that the meeting with Blake would go smoothly.

ARRIVING at Starbucks in Union Square ten minutes to eight, I ordered my drink and breakfast, then found a table in the back. I pulled out my laptop to get some work done before Blake arrived. As I drank my spicy and sweet latte, I started coughing profusely. My drink went down the wrong pipe and probably down my lungs. I was caught off guard seeing Glenn walk toward me. *Seriously? Out of all the Starbucks in the city, he's at this one!*

"Arianna, are you okay? Can I get you anything?"

"I'm." *Cough.* "Fine." *Cough.* "Go." *Cough.* "Away." *Cough.*

"Clearly, you're not okay. You're coughing and can barely talk."

Finally able to catch my breath, the coughing ceased, I took another sip of my drink to coat my throat. "I said I'm fine. Please leave me alone. I thought I made that clear to you the other day."

"I just wanted to ask how Lolo Tony was doing."

"He's fine. Now go."

"Alright." Glenn did the opposite of leaving. He stood there.

"Please just leave me alone and let me be. I don't want to see you again."

"I can't promise that, but I'll leave you alone right now, plus my girlfriend is waiting for me over there." Glenn looked over at the woman picking up two drinks at the counter, then walked out the door of the coffee shop with his girlfriend by his side.

Glenn had the audacity to talk to me in front of the woman he cheated on me with and left me for?! He had serious problems. I glanced down at the time on my phone and it was a quarter past eight. I scanned the room and there was no sign of Blake here. I texted him.

You're late. I thought you wanted to talk. Did you still want to meet?

I waited another ten minutes and he didn't respond to my text. I called his phone, only to have my call go straight to voicemail. I packed up my things. He was the one who wanted to talk. If he can't meet me here, then I'm going to his hotel room.

THE WALK to the Sir Francis Drake Hotel was quick. Starbucks was located on the corner of Powell Street and was right next door to the hotel. There was no excuse for Blake to be late, unless he was with someone last night. *What if I was going to see him with another woman?* It didn't matter. I shouldn't be dating him anyway.

I stood in front of his hotel room and knocked on the door. A minute later, Blake opened the door slightly.

I smiled. "Hey, did you forget? We were supposed to meet at Starbucks at eight o'clock."

"No, I got there but you looked preoccupied," Blake said with a tinge of sarcasm in his voice.

"What? You were the one who wanted to talk. May I please come in? Or is there a woman in your bed right now?"

"What the fuck are you talking about, Arianna? Look!

There's no one else here." Blake's voice got louder. He pulled the door open wider, and I strode through.

He closed the door and followed behind me with his hands on his waist. Blake was dressed in jeans and an olive green pullover sweater that made the green flecks in his hazel eyes pop. He looked delectable, and I wanted to just tear his clothes off his body.

"I'm telling you, Arianna, there is no one else here besides you and me."

I scanned the room, bathroom, and closet, and there wasn't anyone else in here. *Why was I so jealous?* "Alright... well... tell me why you didn't stay at the coffee shop. What do you mean I was preoccupied?"

"I saw you talking to some guy."

"Oh my God, Blake." I rolled my eyes. "That was my ex-boyfriend. He was checking on me because I was choking on my coffee, but I asked him to leave me alone."

"Your ex-boyfriend is in the city? I thought that he was in LA." Blake's stance tensed up. "What the hell is he doing here? Trying to get you ba—"

"For your information, his girlfriend was with him. I don't think he was trying to get back with me. I did *not* appreciate him invading my personal space." I was getting irritated. "What the hell is your problem?"

"My problem? You're the one assuming I have a woman in this room. The only woman who's ever been in here was *you*."

I pulled out sheets of information I printed from the internet search I did on Blake from my bag and flailed them around in front of his face. "I've seen articles, pictures, and heard from people how you really are, Blake Collins. You're a player and a womanizer. You sleep with anyone who has two legs and a pussy. You—"

Before I could say anything further, he walked away. He sat

on the edge of the bed, elbows resting on his thighs, and his head in his hands.

"Arianna, that was my past. You shouldn't believe all that you see, hear, and read. I've changed." He ran his hands through his hair.

"Oh really? The last picture I saw of you with some broad was a week before we met at my lounge."

"Dammit, Arianna! I haven't slept with anyone since my injury two years ago. You're the first and only one I've slept with since. You have to believe me." He looked up at me with pleading eyes.

"I don't know what to believe anymore. Like I mentioned to you before, I am your boss, and we shouldn't be seeing each other." My voice started to quiver. I was so upset and held back my tears. "This is obviously not going to work out. We can't trust each other." Before he can get a word in, I walked out and didn't look back.

I took the long scenic route to work, so I could gather my thoughts and not look like a hot mess when I arrived at head-quarters. I got to the building and literally ran into Elliott as I turned the corner on the way to the elevator. My work tote dropped on the floor as I wobbled backward.

"In a hurry, Arianna?" He grabbed my upper arms, stabi-lizing me and prevented me from falling over.

"Sorry, Elliott. I wasn't paying attention." I stepped back and he let go of my arms. I reached for my bag on the ground, but Elliott swiftly picked it up before I could, then handed it to me. "Thank you."

"How's everything going so far?"

"I think it's going pretty well."

"That's good to hear. How's Tony? Have you visited him?" Elliott looked concerned.

"He's doing therapy and getting better. Thanks for asking."

"He is part of the Storm family, and we hope that he recovers quickly so he can watch one of our games soon."

I smiled. "That would be great."

"What are you doing this morning?"

"Nothing planned. Why do you ask?"

"Let's go to the Storm's practice. They're starting practice shortly. I wanted to introduce you to Blake's private goalie trainer. He just came from Southern California. I think this will improve our odds to make it to playoffs and finally win a Stanley Cup."

"Wow. That sounds great. What time?"

"How about we leave in an hour? I'll let you get settled in your office and catch up on emails before we leave."

"Okay, I'll meet you down here in an hour."

22

BLAKE

My morning didn't go as planned. When do things usually go my way anyway? I planned to see Arianna this morning, so we could talk, instead, I see her with another guy, come to find out it was her ex-boyfriend. Then she came to my hotel room insinuating that I was sleeping with other women before walking out on me. What the fuck?! We're not even together. *But why were we jealous?*

Team practice started in an hour. I decided to get there early so I could release some of this aggression and tension in the gym. On my way to practice, I received a text from Glenn.

Hey, Blake. Our first session didn't get off to a good start. I'll be there during practice today to check out your form while you guys scrimmage. I'll see you in a bit.

Well, I guess he didn't get the hint yesterday. I didn't need or want his help. Dad called me after my first training session with Glenn. He heard that I walked out on the session and I got my ass handed to me. Dad was furious. He yelled at me, saying how much of a disappointment I was to him and to the Collins' name. It was the usual spiel I endured when he was angry with me. I tuned him out, said my "uh-huh's" agreeing with him, and got off the phone with him painlessly.

I arrived at the Bay View Ice Center with thirty minutes of alone time before the rest of the team arrived as well as Glenn. Lifting some weights and jumping rope helped release most of the tension I had brewing inside. My teammates trickled into the locker room and gym slowly. That was my cue to get geared up for practice.

Getting on the ice, I ran some drills with the team before we scrimmaged. We had a game tomorrow evening, and I heavily prepared myself mentally and physically for my first game as a San Francisco Storm goaltender. I needed to focus on my form so my knee didn't get reinjured. I needed to stop thinking about Arianna. Maybe she was right. We shouldn't be dating and seeing each other. We can't be together. Things got complicated and messy... and my life was plenty messy already.

Coach Hall said a few words to us after warming up, informing us that the general manager was stopping by before practice ended to have a meeting with the team. Glenn walked through the double doors before we scrimmaged. He greeted Coach Hall then sat on the bench, observing my skills as I played with my teammates.

Nearing the end of practice, Elliott walked through the doors to the rink. He wasn't alone though. Arianna was walking by his side with her hands clasped in front of her. Her demeanor was pleasant but looked like she meant business. My focus went down the drain as soon as I saw her gorgeous, curvy frame. We made eye contact, and I couldn't stop staring. I watched her greet Coach Hall and the assistant coaches, she waved at the team, then Elliott introduced Arianna to Glenn. From where I stood at the crease, I saw her body tense up and her cheeks turned a couple shades of pink. *Something was wrong.*

Coach blew the whistle. I skated toward the bench where

Arianna was. Their heads turned to look at me as I approached the boards. Seriousness in their faces.

"Mr. Reynolds." I nodded his direction. "Glenn." Nodding at him. "Ms. Santos." I nodded and gazed into her eyes. I could tell something was definitely wrong.

"Mr. Collins, nice to see you again," Elliott said.

"Likewise, sir."

"Blake, you did well today. You kept your glove up," Glenn said with a smirk on his smug face.

"Hello Mr. Collins. It's great to see you," Arianna said, smiling sweetly; however, her eyes didn't say the same. "I just met your personal goalie trainer. It's such a small world. Did you know that Glenn here is my ex-boyfriend?" she said sarcastically.

Elliott's eyes widened. I stiffened up in shock. *What the hell?! Glenn is Arianna's ex-boyfriend?!* He's the same guy who bullied me all through grade school. He's the one who I saw with Arianna at Starbucks this morning. It's official. Today really sucked.

Although I was surprised by the news, I stayed calm and collected before I responded. "Wow. That *is* a small world." Hoping my acting skills weren't too bad and noticeable. "Mr. Reynolds, Coach said you wanted to have a meeting before practice ended. We're ready."

Elliott's facial expression changed. "Yes, that's correct. I'll be right there."

"Well, it was nice seeing you all again." I nodded and skated to where my teammates were.

Shortly after, Elliott met with the team and told us that he felt good about this season and that we needed to continue to stay hungry for the Cup. We all cheered and were pumped for tomorrow's game.

As I skated off the ice to go to the locker room, I turned

around to check on Arianna, but she'd already left... so did Glenn.

BEING the newest player on the team, the Storm Foundation had scheduled me to do community outreach this afternoon. I was visiting the children's floor at Sequoia Grove Hospital. From what I have been told, many of the children there were doing treatments for cancer and other life-threatening illnesses. A couple of the other guys on the team as well as our mascot, Stormer, were going to visit these kids as well.

I went back to my hotel room to drop off my gear, when I received a call from Arianna.

"Hello?"

"Hi, Blake. Are you busy?" she said softly.

"Oh, hey Arianna. I'm not busy. You okay?"

"Not really. I think we need to redo our meetup from this morning. We should talk."

"I don't really have too much to say to you at this point." I sighed. "You should be talking to Glenn, not me."

"Blake—"

I hung up. I couldn't deal with that bullshit and drama today. I had children to visit at the hospital today, and they needed help with brightening up their day. The thought of that warmed my heart. I wanted to bring some hope and optimism into their lives. That's how I got through grade school when I was being bullied and my father was being strict regarding school and hockey growing up. I had a mentor, a teacher, that I looked up to. She helped show me that at the end of the darkness was light. I just needed to be strong.

I took a ride-share to the hospital and met up with the defensemen twins, Zach and Cole Richardson, our captain, Brandon Owens, and left wing Matthew Moore, also known as

Mate in the lobby. I said what's up to them as well as the Storm Foundation staff who brought some gifts for the children.

"Who are we waiting for?" I said to the group.

One of the coordinators from the foundation said, "Miss Santos and our mascot, Stormer."

Dammit! I hung up on Arianna, and now I have to be in the same room with her... again.

Speak of the devil. Stormer, the team's superhero mascot, arrived dressed in black tights, navy blue mask, navy blue Speedo-looking brief, navy and gray fitted long-sleeved shirt with the Storm logo on the front of his chest, and a gray cape with the large logo on his back. Our mascot finished off his costume with navy blue patent leather boots. He had accompanied Arianna from the front door, with her arm through the loop of his. I rolled my eyes, hoping no one saw me.

"Well it looks like we're all here now, let's go up to the third floor," the second coordinator suggested.

We all rode the elevator car together. It was a snug fit, but we fit into one car. I stood on the opposite side of where Arianna was standing. She was facing the elevator door, and I was against the side looking straight at her. Getting out of the elevator was probably amusing to those waiting to get in. It was like a clown car. There were five Storm Foundation staff, five tall and husky hockey players, our short and brawny mascot, and our sexy, curvy owner coming out of the elevator.

Doctors, nurses, and other hospital staff greeted us before we visited each of the children on the floor, taking pictures with them and their families. The look on their faces was priceless. We spoke with the children and each of them told us what they wanted to be when they grew up, what they did while they were here, and what they wanted to do when they finally could go home. There was excitement in their voices. These children were so innocent yet very brave. They were fighting diseases that took over their bodies at such a young age. They told us that they looked up to us and that we were their heroes, but in reality, they were mine.

The last room we visited was of a young boy. He had many tubes and lines attached to him. As I looked around his room, I noticed it was dinosaur-themed.

"I like your room. Do you like dinosaurs?" I asked the child as I knelt down next to him at his bedside.

He nodded 'yes.'

"Which is your favorite dinosaur? Mine is a brontosaurus."

"My favorite is a T. rex... because he's the biggest and strongest," the child said excitedly, then he roared.

"Wow! You sound just like a big dinosaur. T. rex's are so cool. You know who else is strong?"

"Who?"

I pointed to him and touched his nose. "You are."

The little boy had the biggest smile on his face. Then, unexpectedly, he wrapped his arms around my neck and gave me a hug.

I smiled and hugged him back.

WHEN WE FINISHED MAKING our rounds, we went downstairs to the lobby. The coordinators informed us that we were done for the day and could go home. Arianna asked me to stay behind.

"Wait a minute, Blake."

Arianna leaned in closer to my ear, and whispered, "Watching you with these kids melts my heart. And you, of all people, should know how cold my heart really is." She started giggling.

I laughed out loud and leaned into her ear. I said softly, "Oh I do know how icy it truly is, but I have my secret ways to melt it down." I looked into her eyes and winked. "And I changed my mind. I want to talk to you when we're done here."

Arianna looked up at me. She smiled and nodded, acknowledging what I just said. "I'm going to visit my grandfather before going back to the office. Would you like to go with me? You can meet him."

"That sounds good. I would love to meet him."

"Before we go up, I would like to teach you a Filipino tradition that you should do when you meet him. It's called mano."

"Mano," I repeated that Tagalog word.

"That's right. Ma-no." Arianna slowly pronounced it again. "Mano is an honoring-gesture in the Filipino culture, where it is performed as a sign of respect to our elders. It's also a way of receiving a blessing from our elders." She grabbed my hand. "Pretend you're my grandfather." Then she bowed and pressed her forehead on the back of my hand. "Then you say *mano po*. Now you try it."

I followed what Arianna just did using her hand and I said, "Mano po."

"Perfect. You're ready to meet Lolo Tony." She smiled, her eyes sparkled.

Arianna and I went up to the fifth level. She and I checked in with the nurse and went into his room. Arianna knocked on the door and peeked inside.

"Hi, Lolo Tony, how are you?" Arianna said as she walked in. He was lying in bed with his head propped up as he watched television. Arianna leaned in and kissed his cheek. "Lolo, I have someone I would like you to meet. He is the newest goalie for the Storm."

I was standing in the hallway outside his room. Arianna gestured for me to come inside.

"Lolo Tony, this is Blake Collins... Blake, this is my grandfather, Tony Santos, Sr."

I stood next to Tony's bed and bowed, while grabbing his hand, I pressed my forehead against the back of it. "Mano po." I stood up. "It's very nice to meet you, Mr. Santos."

Arianna smiled proudly. Tony had a crooked smile, but he smiled regardless. That made me so happy.

Our visit was short. Arianna and I told her grandfather what we did as part of the Storm Foundation's community outreach. He seemed pleased.

"Thank you for visiting, anak. I'm so very proud of you." Tony told his granddaughter. "Blake, please take care of my Ari and help her with the franchise. You two make a great team."

I was surprised at his words and advice. "I will, sir. Ari is very special and I will take care of her for you as well as the team." Arianna looked at me as she held her grandfather's hand. Tears welled up in her eyes and the corners of her mouth lifted.

What I responded with was true. I wanted to take care of Arianna and help her with the franchise. It was a matter of whether Arianna was willing to accept that from me.

23

ARIANNA

Watching Blake interact with the children at the hospital and with Lolo Tony made my heart burst. I saw a different side of Blake. Not the womanizer that the media portrayed him to be. He truly cared and wanted to help. Even though we've only known each other a short while, I've never seen that side of him. It was adorable.

After our visit with Lolo Tony, I needed to get back to the office. I looked down at my watch.

"It's three-thirty already?! I'm sorry, Blake. I didn't mean to keep you from any plans you had this afternoon."

"It's all good. I didn't have much going on."

"Where are you headed to now?"

"Probably back to the hotel."

"I drove my daddy's car. Need a lift back to the hotel?"

"Sure, why not. Thank you, Ari."

I smiled at Blake.

"By the way, I think your nickname 'Ari' is cute. Why didn't you tell me about it?"

"Well, we never had a chance to really talk and get to know each other wel—"

"How about now? Do you want to go back to your office and talk? Maybe I can teach you more hockey?"

"That sounds great, Blakey." I slyly grinned.

"Blakey? Hmm... I like it." He laughed.

On the car ride to headquarters, we talked about my large Filipino family and traditions we had, growing up in the Bay Area, and my best friends. He talked about his family, growing up in Canada, and his passion for hockey. We had a real conversation. No flirting. Just real talk.

"So this is your father's car?"

"Yeah, mine is still in SoCal. I think I'm going to fly into LAX early this weekend to grab more belongings, visit Blue Velvet Lounge to check on them, and drive back in my car."

"No shit. I was planning to do the same thing minus visiting Blue Velvet Lounge, but I can do that too." He laughed.

"Do you want to fly down together on Saturday morning and drive back up on Sunday afternoon?"

"Yeah, that would be fun." I could see from my peripheral vision that Blake was smiling.

WE ARRIVED AT MY OFFICE, and I pushed the door behind us to close.

"Would you like anything to drink, Blake?" I asked him as I walked toward the wet bar area in my office.

"Water would be good if you have any." Blake sat down on one side of the black leather couch positioned near the wet bar.

"Yes... catch." I threw a water bottle toward him from my mini-fridge. Of course, he caught it as any good goalie would have done.

"Thanks... so... we should talk about everything... honestly."

"We should." I sat down on the other end of the couch with my bottled water. I turned my body facing him, my back resting on the armrest, my legs bent and feet on the couch. "What do you want to talk about first?"

"Well, for starters, Glenn is your ex-boyfriend?"

"Yes, Glenn was my longtime on-again, off-again boyfriend. He left me for another woman, someone he cheated on me with for years. He was my high school sweetheart, or so I thought." I looked down at my hands. "I didn't realize until the day he left me, how much of a toxic relationship I was in. Glenn manipulated me, controlled me, and emotionally abused me."

Blake's hand squeezed the water bottle he held tightly. He was getting upset with all the information I disclosed to him.

"I can't believe how someone could treat you like that for many years, and that you allowed it."

"He was my first everything. I didn't know what a relationship should be like. We fought all the time. I thought that was normal in relationships."

"Thank you for sharing this with me... but I need to tell you something about Glenn. I'm sure you're aware that he was born and raised in Canada. Well..." Blake took a deep breath in and exhaled.

I can see in his demeanor that this was hard for him, but I waited patiently.

"Glenn bullied me pretty much the entire time I was in grade school. He tormented and threatened me. I didn't want to go to school, but my father, being the asshole he was, made me go. He didn't listen to me when I told him what was going on, and he told me to 'grow up and be a big boy.' I was only eight years old when this started."

I listened to him and felt empathy. I imagined young Blake being bullied by young Glenn.

Blake went on, "I hated Glenn. So when I saw him for the first time in years and found out that he was hired as my personal goalie trainer, I was so pissed off. I even walked out on him during our first session."

"Oh, Blake. I'm so sorry."

"Don't be sorry. I survived. I buried all those memories, but they rushed back as soon as I saw him again."

"Well, let's change the subject, and talk about your dating history. From what I've heard and seen online and in social media, you're a player... always with different women..."

"Yes, I *was* like that. But as I mentioned to you, that was before my knee injury. After I got injured, I stopped dating and sleeping with anyone because I was focused on healing and getting back on the ice."

"All the women in those pictures were tall, beautiful, and looked like models." My voice quivered. "I am the total opposite of them. The token minority woman. I am—" My head dropped low and I felt ashamed for bringing it up.

Blake scooted closer to me and placed his hand on my knee, tilted his head, and searched for my eyes. "You are gorgeous, both inside and out. And the reason I enjoy being with you is not because of the color of your skin, it's the way you make me feel."

I lifted my head up, gazed into his eyes, seeking validity in his statement.

"I kept telling myself that we shouldn't be seeing each other; that this was a risk for both of our careers... but I can't stop thinking of you. No other woman has made me feel the way you do... and I want more. I know that sounds selfish—"

I placed my hand on top of his. "If it's selfish, then I'm greedy too. I want you and no one else," I said softly.

"So... what does this mean?"

"I guess we won't be seeing other people?" My brows furrowed in curiosity as I eagerly awaited his response.

"I guess not." Blake grinned, then took my hand and placed a small kiss on the back of it.

We established that we wouldn't be dating anyone else except for one another. We just had to think of how and when we would see each other. With his games and being on the road, we needed to schedule our secret time together.

Blake sat there quietly with a wicked grin on his face.

"What are you thinking about?" I asked him.

"Nothing, really." He still had that smile slapped on his face.

"What's making you smile? Come on, tell me." I sat up and crossed my legs Indian-style. With a smile like that on Blake's face, he must be thinking of something naughty.

"Well… I was just fantasizing how it would be to fuck you here in your office. I thought about that the first time I visited here. Do you ever think about that?"

I laughed. "That's cute."

"Cute?"

"Yes, it's cute that you fantasize about us… to answer your question, yes, I have thought about it. The day you came to my office for the first time; I was sitting behind my desk and you were sitting in the chair in front of me. All I kept thinking about was you eating me out from under the desk."

Blake turned his head and raised an eyebrow. "Really?" he asked in a sexy voice.

I smiled back devilishly and winked at him.

"You know that I can help make that fantasy come true." Blake stood up and held a hand out. "I want to help fulfill all your desires, beautiful."

I took his hand and stood up. I swung my arms around his waist, placing my cheek on his chest, hearing his heartbeat. "Handsome, you're amazing. I want to do the same for you."

Blake wrapped his arms around my shoulder and tightened the embrace. I loosened my hold, tilted my head up to look at him. He looked down at me and kissed my lips gently. He held my hand and directed me to my desk.

I stopped, pulling Blake back a bit. "I hate to do this, but can I get a rain check on tonight please?"

"Of course. Is everything alright?"

"Not really, my stomach is cramping and I don't feel too well." I grimaced, holding my stomach.

"Can I get you anything to help you?" Blake's expression filled with concern.

"It's okay, Blakey. I can drop you off at your hotel and head home to rest if that's okay."

"Of course, Ari."

24

BLAKE

I woke up with the biggest grin on my face. Arianna and I talked through everything yesterday, and it didn't seem like we had any more lingering issues. We made up. I smirked just thinking about it. Things were perfect with Arianna right now, and I didn't want to mess things up. She dropped me off at the hotel last night before heading home to rest. I felt bad. She wasn't feeling well and I couldn't help her.

When we put everything on the table, I brought up Glenn working closely with me. We both felt that it was super awkward, not to mention, I just don't like the guy. I wanted to smash his face every time I saw him, even more so now that I knew he was Arianna's ex-boyfriend. All the pain he put her through all those years, we didn't need him here as a reminder of our pasts. We needed him to leave. Arianna said she would talk to Elliott and have him cancel Glenn's contract. I guess it worked. Glenn sent me a message this morning:

Hey, Blake. I have been transferred to another assignment. It was good working with you and good luck with tonight's game.

I responded to Glenn by thanking him. Keeping it short and

to the point. I didn't need to engage in any more conversations with him. He was a distraction.

It was game day. I was hyped, my head was clear, and I was mentally focused on tonight's game against the Seattle Renegade. Two years ago, playing against them cost me a knee injury that I will have to deal with for the rest of my life. It affected how I played and I continued the rehabilitation for that injury up to now. But nonetheless, I was ready for them.

Finally, getting out of the warmth of my bed, I received another text message. This time it was from my gorgeous girl.

Good morning, handsome. Yesterday was great. I can't wait to watch you crush the Renegade tonight. I'll be watching from the suite at the arena. Good luck! Missing you already! Xo

Arianna was going to watch the game? Sweet! Come to think of it, this will be her first game as the owner of the Storm. I'm definitely going to make her proud. I responded back to her.

Good morning, beautiful. I had a great time with you last night too. I'm going to make you proud tonight. I'll be playing for you. Then we can celebrate tonight at the hotel or if you prefer, your office. I miss you too! Xo

I'm even more pumped about the game tonight, knowing that the one that holds my heart will be watching. I looked at the time and needed to get ready for morning skate. I felt that today would be a good one.

MORNING SKATE WAS QUICK. I ran a couple drills and worked on some things that Coach Hall critiqued me on.

"Great practice, Blake. You ready for tonight's game?" Coach asked as we walked down the hall to the locker room.

"Yeah, I'm ready, Coach. This is my first game as a Storm, and I'm not going to let you or the team down tonight."

"That's what I like to hear. We're ready for a comeback. Now that you're part of the team, we'll be unstoppable." Coach patted my back as I entered the locker room first.

"Thanks, Coach."

I cooled down in the gym, took a shower, and got ready for the day. I went back to the hotel, thinking about texting Arianna to see if she wanted to go out to lunch, but I decided not to. I didn't want to risk anyone seeing us during the day. That's where rumors start, and we didn't need that right now. I just grabbed something for lunch from the deli that was down the street from where I stayed and brought it back to my room. I placed it on the desk and pulled out the black leather executive chair and sat down.

I texted Arianna anyway just to let her know that I was thinking about her. She responded back right away with a selfie. She was by her office window, with the Bay Bridge in the background. Her face was breathtaking. She made a cute kissing gesture with her dark pink juicy lips.

I can't stop thinking about you, handsome. Can't wait to see you tonight! I'll make sure to wear something extra special. Xo

Just thinking about what she might have on, or not, tonight while she watched me play got me horny and hard. I licked my lips, then texted her back.

You're so gorgeous! Thank you for the picture, beautiful! Now I can't stop thinking about what you'll be wearing... or not wearing. Dammit, woman! What are you doing to me?

The hardness of my cock pressed up against my jeans, making it uncomfortable. I unzipped my pants and released my erection. I couldn't help but stare at the picture of Arianna. She was so sexy and I couldn't believe she was mine. I stroked my length, thinking of her sucking the tip with her full luscious lips, then going deeper in her mouth. I closed my eyes and stroked a little faster. My breath hitched.

I thought of the times I bottomed out on Arianna, hearing her moan and calling out my name. My cock throbbed, blood rushing to the crown. Firming my grip on my erection, I pumped my cock even faster. I opened my eyes and gazed at her picture again. My balls were full of cream, and I was ready to explode. I groaned as I got closer to the edge. Sweat beaded down my forehead. My heart rate increased, and my breathing became shallower. I felt like I was nearing my release. I closed my eyes and growled as my length tensed up, then I emptied my load all over my hand.

I opened my eyes and slowed down my breathing. That was one way to satisfy my thirst for Arianna. I looked down at my hand that was still gripping my length, got up from the chair, and went straight to the bathroom to get cleaned up. I changed out of my clothes and stayed in boxers until I needed to get suited up for tonight's game.

I ARRIVED at SV Communications Arena an hour earlier than we were scheduled to be here. It was my ritual to get some alone time to warm up in the gym, tape up my sticks, and get mentally prepared for tonight's game. My knee wasn't bothering me so far, but I decided that I needed to tape it anyway for extra relief and precautions. I didn't want to chance my knee being reinjured.

As the rest of my teammates slowly arrived at the arena, the players went directly into the locker room to get ready. Each player had their own routine and pregame ritual. I stayed focused and did some drills to help with eye-hand coordination and my speed. Coach arrived and met with us, giving us an inspirational speech and advice on what to watch out for when playing against our opponents, the Seattle Renegade.

I had all my pads and gear on and was ready for action. We

walked into the tunnel toward the entrance of the rink where the Storm would go in. I was the guy leading the team onto the ice because tonight, I was the starting goalie. Before the game began, my teammates approached me and tapped on my pads for good luck. When the last player tapped my pads, I got settled in the crease, then the arena announcer introduced the starting players for tonight's game.

"And for your starting goaltender for tonight's game, number thirty-one, Blake Collins." The announcer's voice was animated. There was a loud roar from the crowd. I was surprised since I was just traded, but I was happy to have some fans already.

I looked up toward the presidential suite in the arena and could see a silhouette of a curvaceous figure standing up and looking down. *There's my girl.* I whispered to myself, "This one's for you, Ari."

After the National Anthem was performed, it was game time.

Ksssh-Ksssh-Ksssh. The sounds of blades cutting the ice, and the slapping of hockey sticks against one another as the players tried to get the puck. I stayed sharp and focused on where the puck was and who had it. I wasn't going to let anyone get that puck into my net.

After a grueling three periods, the game was scoreless for both the Storm and Renegade. We were in overtime and we needed to win. I wanted this win... and so did Arianna. The loud buzzer echoed at the end of the OT. Now it was time for a shootout. Coach Hall picked #88 Captain Brandon Owens, and the Richardson twins - #12 Zachary "Zach" Richardson and #22 Nicholas "Cole" Richardson to play. It was a great choice considering they all had great skills. The Renegades chose #8 - Benjamin "Benji" Rice, #42 - Nathan "Nate" Cook, and #26 - Robert "Robbie" Webb to do the shootout.

We had home team advantage and Coach Hall decided that

the Storm would go first in the shootout. Coach Hall assigned Zach to go first. Zach gained speed, faked to the left, and scored. Next up was the Renegades. Their coach chose #42 Cook to go first. Cook skated toward me in a zigzag form. I followed his motion and anticipated his next move. He took a shot and I raised my glove up for a save. Brandon went next, and he slapped one hard into the net from the side. Next up is #26 Webb from the opposing team. I got into my stance and skated from side-to-side, mimicking Webb's movements. Webb shot, I moved to my right and landed on my knees, but the puck deflected from the goal post. It didn't go in.

The loud roar from the crowd rumbled through the arena. I stood up as all of my teammates skated out on the ice to congratulate me individually for a good game. They each touch their helmet with mine. This game was the best one I'd ever played. I was so proud of being part of the San Francisco Storm. After celebrating our win on the ice, one of the Storm staff stopped me and told me to sign one of the pucks to throw to one of the fans. I was being acknowledged as one of the "Stars of the Game." The other two 'stars' were Brandon and Zach.

The announcer hyped up the crowd. "For your #1 Star of the Game, it's your own San Francisco Storm #31 Blake Collins." I skated around the rink with my stick up, stopped to the glass, and tossed the puck to a child standing behind the glass. I smiled and skated away to the locker room.

I arrived at the locker room shortly after, where I found Arianna doing a press interview out in the hallway. This was the first time she spoke in public and to the media as the new owner of the Storm. I smiled as I walked by. I heard Arianna say, "This is a very exciting time for the Storm. The team worked hard. This was a great game." She was coached by the Storm's public relations team on what to say during interviews. The players have also been taught the do's and don'ts of what to say during press interviews.

I sat on the locker room bench after removing my gear. My hair was drenched in sweat, I hung a towel around my neck, and I was waiting for the media to leave before getting into the shower. The reporters came to talk to me last as I was the last one in the locker area.

"Blake, how does it feel to be a Storm?" a reporter from ESPN asked me.

"It's exciting. The fans were great. The excitement level was through the roof tonight," I stated.

"How did you feel shutting out your first game as a Storm?" another reporter asked from a local news station.

"Well, it felt great. Everyone contributed during tonight's game. We kept pushing and played hard," I told him.

After a few more questions, the reporters were escorted out and I finally jumped into the shower and got dressed. I looked at the time on my phone and saw that it was eleven o'clock at night. It was pretty late and I wasn't sure if Arianna still wanted to meet tonight. She probably left to go home already.

A couple minutes later, I received a text from her.

Great game, handsome! Are you almost done getting ready? I'm actually in the garage waiting in my car. I think you deserve something special for the impressive moves I saw on the ice tonight. Xo

Arianna was still here, and she was waiting for me. She was the one I was most impressed with. I responded to her message.

Thanks, beautiful! I am almost done. I'll see you shortly. I can think of some impressive moves I can show you off the ice. Xo

I was the last one out of the locker room. The rest of the guys went out to celly at a lounge, club, or went home to their families. I walked into the garage. Arianna's car was one of the few cars left parked there. I slid into the passenger seat, closed the door, and gave her a long, deep kiss.

"I missed you, beautiful."

25

ARIANNA

Last night was the first time that I felt so proud to be the owner of the San Francisco Storm. For someone who didn't know the game that well, I was blown away. The game was exciting and Blake was playing his best. He said he was playing for me. I believed him.

As the new owner of the Storm, Elliott and the public relations team thought it would be best to do a press interview after my first game as the new owner. I thought I did a good job with the interviews. I was happy that the Storm won. It made for a better interview. I received questions that were as simple as "How do you feel being the new owner of the Storm?" to complex ones "How does it feel to be the only female owner in the NHL?" and "Being that you are a minority and a female, do you think you will be treated differently in this sport where it's primarily dominated by men?"

Luckily my public relations squad taught me well and I had an answer for everything, whether the press liked it or not. My responses included, "It was a great game. This is an exciting time for the franchise," "Being a female doesn't matter as long as I put in the same hard work as anyone else would to make this organization successful. I am well-educated and can pick up on things quickly," and "I expect to be treated differently because I know I'm different, but I will put in the hard work and prove that I have a right to be here. The NHL should have a place for everyone in the league."

I waited for Blake to finish getting ready after the game. I didn't want to text him until I knew the media had left the locker room and finished interviews. I didn't want to take a chance that people would see Blake and me together. Mine was the only car left in the garage. My windows were tinted so it would be difficult to see if there was someone in the car. I saw Blake in the rearview mirror walking toward my car. I unlocked the door. He put his bag on the back seat, climbed in the passenger side, and gave me a long, deep kiss that took my breath away. *Wow! How did I get so lucky?*

"Hello to you too, handsome." I gave Blake a devilish grin.

"Hi, beautiful. Want to go to the hotel?" he asked in a low, sexy voice.

"Yes, sounds like a great idea."

"Did you want to grab something to eat before we get to the room?"

"Can we order room service?"

"Of course. Anything you want."

"There's definitely something I want." I made my voice as seductive as I could.

I turned my head to look at Blake quickly, and his eyes were blazing with desire with one brow up. I knew what he wanted because I wanted it too. I wanted him.

WE ARRIVED at his room at the Sir Francis Drake. As soon as we entered the room, he closed and locked the door behind him. We dropped our bags onto the ground and madly kissed on the lips. We hadn't seen each other for a day, but it seemed like a week.

We quickly stripped off our clothes. There was an urgency to our desire since I was the one who asked for a rain check, which I regretted. I craved his touch and kisses, and lusted for him to claim my lips and body. We didn't want to waste any time. Our hands caressed all over each other's body. I reached down to take his length in my hand, but he stepped back.

"Last time you had your way with me, this time it's my turn, beautiful." His voice was soft and sensual.

Blake took my hand and escorted me to his bed. "Lie down," he commanded.

"Yes, sir," I said in a sultry voice. I laid on the bed as instructed.

Blake hovered above me, leaning in to kiss me on my lips. He followed with a path of kisses down my neck, then he reveled in flicking and sucking my perky nipples, alternating between each breast. Blake took his time trailing kisses down my body to my navel. He caressed my inner thighs with his hands, spreading my legs open. Then he pulled apart my wet folds uncovering my swollen pink clit. I let out a soft moan.

"Mmmm. I can't get enough of hearing you moan for me." He smirked. "You're so wet already." My sex was soaked with fluid.

He leaned in, quickly flicking his warm tongue on my clit, then he sucked on my pleasure center. Sounds of him puckering on my sex as he sucked turned me on. *Oh my fucking God!* He definitely knew how to eat me out. "Ohhh! Fuuuck!"

Blake continued alternating between flicking and sucking. I arched my back and clenched the bedsheet with my fists.

"Fuck." I exhaled sharply. My respiration and heartbeat increased as he devoured my sex. I was reaching my climax until he slid his middle finger into my opening and pulled back, teasing me. I let out another moan. "You're such a tease."

I could feel a mischievous grin on his face as he flicked his tongue in circles around my swollen nub. He groaned. Then he plunged his finger all the way in. A bellow of delight expelled out of me.

"I'm going to come." My breathing quickened and the sounds of my moans got louder as I got closer to my peak. My back arched again and my hands raked through his hair, then I pressed the back of his head to my pussy as my body jerked, releasing all the pleasure that flowed through my body.

Blake stood up, standing by the edge of the bed then he flipped me around, my stomach on the bed.

"I want to fuck you from behind, gorgeous." His voice sexy and smoldering.

I turned my face to the side, my cheek laid against the mattress as I got on my knees and pushed my ass up in the air.

"You have a nice ass." I caught him staring at my plump ass and he licked his lips.

Blake spread my ass cheeks open and gave my pussy one more lick and suck. I moaned as an electric current of pleasure hit every nerve ending in my body. His swollen head grazed my opening, slowly finding the entrance to my sex.

Then he thrust his thick, hard cock in, filling my tight, wet sex with all of him. I drew a breath in sharply. Blake plunged his length into me until he bottomed out. I let out a low groan of pure pleasure. He slid in and out at a rhythmic pace, holding my waist as he penetrated me from behind.

"Fuuuuccck." He growled. He picked up speed in his gyrations. His jewels slapping against my pussy. He leaned forward, wrapping his arm around my stomach. He fucked me hard and with determination to make me come again. His hand on my stomach moved lower to my sex and he rubbed my clit in a circular motion.

"Oh fuuucckkk, Blake!" I screamed. I pressed myself against the bed, lowering my chest and raising my ass up higher.

Blake growled. My walls were swelling up around his throbbing cock as he pushed inside my pussy, getting closer to my climax. My hands were gripping the blankets tighter.

"Fuck! I'm coming," I shrieked. Pleasure surged through my vagina. Having him inside me felt so good and so right. I reached my peak and let out a loud moan. "Oh fuck," I said, coming down from my orgasmic high.

Soon after, Blake jerked quickly and with force against my sex. "Fuuuuccck, Ari!" He gave a hard thrust inside me and his body shuddered. He lay limp on my back, his cock still inside me. We lay still for a minute, slowing our breath down from our amazing night.

Blake pulled out from me and rolled to the side, lying next to me. I rolled to my side, facing him. My head lay on my hand as I propped up on my elbow, staring at Blake with a smitten look on my face.

"Arianna, do you know how amazing you are?"

"You've told me a few times, but I don't mind hearing it again." I gave him a big smile.

"You're so fucking amazing. I can't get enough of you and I only want you."

I was so happy to hear that, to know he felt that way about me. I wasn't just a fling to him, I was *his.*

"I think you're so amazing. I don't want to be with anyone else except you."

26

ARIANNA

Monday morning, Elliott stopped me in passing at Storm headquarters. He was coming out of the elevator as I was going in. I told the other Storm executives riding the elevator that they could go ahead and I'd catch the next one.

"Good morning, Arianna. How was your weekend?" Elliott asked.

"Good morning, Elliott. It was productive. How was yours?"

"It was wonderful. Thanks for asking. Look, Arianna, I need to meet with you later this afternoon. Do you have time to meet with me?"

"Yeah, sure. Is everything okay? What did you need to discuss?" I tilted my head to the side, concerned there was an issue with the franchise.

"I'm fine. It's personal, so I would rather talk to you later in private."

I looked at my phone's calendar at today's schedule. "Oh, okay. I'm free at two o'clock. Does that work for you?"

"Perfect. I'll see you in your office at two o'clock."

"Bye, Elliott."

BLAKE WAS on the road for the next couple days. He will be coming back to the Bay Area on Thursday evening. This was the longest we've been apart since we talked about our insecurities with one another and hashed things out. I was in meetings all morning, which kept me occupied and my mind off Blake. I missed him so much.

I texted Blake during my lunch break. I needed to hear that he was good, and that they'd made it to their destination in Seattle, Washington, then they were headed to Canada, specifically to Vancouver, British Columbia. Blake mentioned last night when we were cuddling in bed, that he was excited to go back home to Vancouver, so he could visit his mom and sister. Blake was not too keen on seeing his father again, but I convinced him that he only has one father and that he should feel blessed that he's still living. He told me that he knew I was right.

Hi handsome. I miss you so much! Have you guys made it to Washington already? Is it Thursday yet? I don't know how much longer I can be without you next to me in bed. Xo

I brought my lunch to work today: pancit bihon and lumpia. I had a craving for home-cooked Filipino food and was happy that Lola Lynn cooked these egg rolls and a noodle dish last night. She visited Lolo Tony every day in the hospital. I didn't know how she even had time to cook, but I was grateful nonetheless that she still cooked for Daddy and me. You know they love you when your family is concerned with how thick you're getting but yet continue to tell you to keep eating. It didn't make sense, but that's how my Filipino family was. It bothered me when I was younger, but now, I just ignored it.

A couple minutes later, I received a text from Blake. I got excited to hear from him.

Hi, beautiful. We actually just made it to Seattle. Of

course, it's raining as usual. **I miss you and wish we were still in bed. I'll FaceTime you later tonight. Xo**

Our first FaceTime session! I can't wait! I had a huge grin on my face thinking of all the different things the call could lead to. My cheeks heated up. I was blushing thinking of Blake and what I wanted to do to him. I wanted to please Blake and remind him who he would be coming home to.

My thoughts were interrupted by a knocking on my door. Why didn't my secretary notify me by phone that I had a visitor? *She was probably still at lunch.* I glanced at the clock and it was ten minutes to two o'clock.

"Come in," I said out loud, hoping it was enough volume for the visitor to hear.

The door swung open, and Elliott briskly walked through. His stride was confident and his demeanor was serious.

"Elliott." I stood up from behind my desk and turned off the screen from my phone.

"Arianna, I know I'm early, but wanted to talk to you."

"Please sit down."

We both sat down across from one another at my desk. I pushed my lunch to the side.

"I didn't mean to interrupt you during lunch."

"It's fine. I was pretty much done. So, what did you want to talk to me about?"

"How's Tony doing?"

"Well, he seems to be doing better. After the Storm Foundation Children's Hospital visit yesterday, Blake and I went to visit my grandfather. He was in good spirits and enjoyed talking hockey with Blake."

"Oh, he's met Blake?"

"Yes, Blake wanted to meet the man who gave the Storm to me. Is that a problem?"

"Let me ask you this. Are you and Blake dating? I heard some chatter that you two have been spending a lot of time with one another."

"We're not dating. You told us to work together so Blake can teach me about hockey. That's what we've been doing."

"You're lying, Arianna."

"Excuse me? I don't appreciate being called a liar in my own office. I *am* still your boss, and I can fire you for disrespecting me."

"Go ahead... fire me, but I wouldn't do that if I were you. I have proof that you and Blake are more than just colleagues."

"There is nothing going on between Blake and me."

Elliott pulled out his cell phone from his pocket and scrolled through, looking for something.

I had always been careful when meeting with Blake. So I'm not sure what Elliott's going to show me.

"This is a video of when Blake took you to Bay View Ice Center for the first time. He asked me if he could teach you about hockey at the practice rink after hours. I couldn't deny him access, so instead, I checked the cameras to see what you guys were up to."

I saw on Elliott's phone screen a video of Blake and me on the ice. I was wobbling as I tried to skate. Blake guided me before I could fall, then we kissed. *Why was Elliott doing this?*

Elliott scrolled through his phone again and showed me pictures of Blake getting into my car and of Blake and I kissing after the Storm game last night.

"I'm going to ask you again. Are you and Blake in a relationship?"

"I don't know. Why does it matter?" Blood was rushing to my head. Annoyance in my tone.

"Well, whatever you two have going on needs to stop... now." Elliott didn't hesitate. He was straight to the point. "You're going to end the relationship with him."

"What?! Why?!" In shock, I sat still, trying to absorb the information.

"This will cause negative publicity for the franchise. Your career and reputation will be ruined as well as your boyfriend's. Do you want to end Blake's career?"

I looked away. "No, of course not," I said softly.

"Good. Well, the reason I wanted to meet with you was to tell you that I was going over the financial report from last quarter and last month, and it's not doing well. I think we should schedule a meeting with the CFO, board members, and executives to come up with a plan sooner rather than later, before the new year and definitely before the end of the season."

"When you say 'it's not doing well,' how bad is it?"

"We'll be in the red soon."

"Okay, we need to have an emergency board meeting ASAP. I'll have my assistant schedule it for tomorrow. I didn't become the new owner just to have us go bankrupt."

"Alright, Arianna. I'll wait to hear from your assistant then."

"Thanks for the update, Elliott."

"You're welcome." Elliott walked out of my office.

I've spent the last few days thinking about Blake, so much that I forgot about running the organization as a business. There is money involved and employees relying on paychecks to bring home for their families.

I dialed my secretary on the office line.

"Hi, can you please schedule an emergency board meeting with the CFO, GM, board members, and executive staff for tomorrow at ten o'clock in the morning sharp? I also need the finance department to send me the last twelve month's financial reports and the last annual report for the franchise. I need it in an hour. Thank you."

It was going to be a long night.

AFTER A FEW HOURS at the office, I went home super exhausted and stressed. My mind was drained, trying to process all the financial information before the meeting I had with the board tomorrow. Daddy and Kuya Eric were sitting in the living room watching a movie when I arrived home.

"Arianna, anak. How was work?" Daddy asked as I closed the front door.

I walked over to the living room and gave my dad a kiss on the cheek. "Wish I could say it went well, but I'm so stressed out right now. I have an important meeting tomorrow."

"I left your dinner in the fridge."

"I think I'm going to take a shower and go to bed."

"Ari, do you need help with anything?" Kuya Eric asked.

At that moment, I suddenly couldn't think. I was gasping for air, my heartbeat was racing, and I felt like the room was spinning. I nearly fell over, but Daddy stood up quickly and grabbed me for support. Kuya Eric brought a chair over and I sat down. I was having a panic attack. I hadn't had one in a while. The last one I could remember was when Glenn broke up with me the first time. I was lost then and didn't know what to do.

I couldn't think, focus, or breathe. I was losing myself again.

27

BLAKE

"**B**lake, you're home! Melissa, your brother is here!" my mother yelled as she ran out the front door of the house as I strolled through the driveway. She gave me a kiss on the cheek and a long, tight hug. "I've missed you, honey."

"I've missed you too, Mom," I said softly in her ear as we embraced.

Soon after, Melissa came out of the house. "Hey, Blake!" She wrapped her arms around me after Mom finally released me from her bear hug. Who knew a five-foot-four-inch woman could have so much strength to knock the wind out of me with a hug.

"Hey, Mel. How've you been, eh?" We released our embrace and walked to go inside the house.

"I've been good. I've been following most of your games when I'm not scheduled at the hospital."

"Oh, nice! Thanks!" I cheerfully said as I wrapped my arm around my little sister's shoulder. "How's work? Delivering lots of babies lately?"

"It's busy. Yeah, lots of babies born this week. I'm waiting for you to have one so I can finally be an aunt and spoil the kid."

"I would, but I don't have a wife or girlfriend to have one with."

"Well, hurry up. You're not getting any younger."

I rolled my eyes and tightened my hold to bring my sister closer to me. "I've missed you, Mel." I laughed out loud.

We entered the house I grew up in. It hasn't changed too much except they renovated it a bit to make it look more modern. There were new hardwood floors, kitchen appliances, and couches. Our family and school pictures were still hung on the walls in the same spot as when I moved out of the house a few years ago. This house still gave me all the feels of the comfort of home. Mom does her best to make the house look good all the time, in case visitors stopped by unexpectedly.

The floor was creaking from the stairwell. Heavy footsteps were getting louder with each step going down the stairs slowly. Then there he was in front of me. My dad.

"Hello, son." He stuck his hand out. Melissa and Mom left for the kitchen so Dad and I could be alone.

"Hey, Dad." I took his hand and firmly gave it a shake.

Dad never really showed any compassion to Melissa and me growing up. I didn't remember receiving any hugs or hearing 'I love you.' All I remembered was Dad being strict on us with our studies, extra-curricular activities, and for me, with hockey... especially hockey.

"Are you planning on staying here for the night?" Dad asked.

"No, just visiting. I'm going back to the hotel later tonight with the rest of the team." *Plus I'm supposed to FaceTime with Arianna later and want to be alone when we video chat.*

"Are you ready for the game against Vancouver Thunder tomorrow night, eh?"

"Yes—"

"Because I know you haven't been training with the private

trainer I asked Mr. Reynolds to hire for you. I heard that the new owner of the Storm is the reason why the trainer got fired."

"That's not true, sir."

"The franchise is going to shit with a female owner. She probably doesn't know anything about hockey. I saw her on television being interviewed and she is—"

"She is a businesswoman... a hard worker, and professional. I think she'll do a great job with the Storm organization." My words were curt and I didn't appreciate how Dad was talking about Arianna. He hasn't even met her or gotten to know her.

"You've only been here not even fifteen minutes and you're disrespecting your father." His voice was getting louder.

"Dad, I'm trying not to argue with you. I was just telling you that Arianna is not bad. She is settling in—"

"Arianna? You address her on a first name basis?"

"Yes, we became friends."

"Hmm." Dad raised one of his eyebrows and pursed his lips.

"Is there something wrong with being friends with her?"

"No, but don't get too comfortable. You never know what the future holds for you."

"Yes, sir." *What the hell does he mean by that?*

―――――――――――

FOR THE REST of the evening and during dinner, Dad didn't say a word. He ate dinner and headed upstairs. I didn't even have a chance to say goodbye to him. I went back to the hotel in downtown Vancouver after dinner. I texted Arianna on the way to the hotel.

Hi, beautiful. I'm on my way back to the hotel from my parents' house. I look forward to seeing you on our call. I miss you! Xo

After twenty minutes, I didn't get a response from her. I hoped everything was okay. I haven't heard from her since lunchtime. I settled in my hotel room and changed into a shirt and boxers. Lying in bed, I flipped the channels on the television. Why hasn't she called me yet? I was getting worried about Arianna. I texted her again.

Hey, beautiful. I miss seeing your face and hearing your voice. Are we still going to FaceTime?

Still no response from Arianna. I called her and it went straight to voicemail. I left a message for her to call or text me back to tell me she was okay. Maybe her battery died, and she has no way of charging it. I was trying to think of scenarios that didn't have her in any type of danger.

Then my phone rang. I looked at the caller ID and it said *Private*.

"Hello?"

"Hey, Blake, it's Elliott Reynolds."

"Oh hey, Mr. Reynolds. What can I help you with?"

"I know you're on the road, but I'm going to keep this short. You've been traded back to LA. Someone from the Crusaders will be contacting you. Good luck, Blake."

Then the call dropped. Elliott hung up the call.

What the fuck?! I got traded within a week?!

A few minutes later, I received another call.

"Hey, Blake Collins. This is Sam Cunningham, the general manager for the Crusaders."

"Hello, Mr. Cunningham."

"I'm sure you've heard, but you're coming back to LA. We're happy to have you back."

"With all due respect, sir, I thought I was a liability to the team. I'm confused as to why I'm returning if you didn't want me last week."

"Listen, son, this is the way the league works. You may never know, you could be traded again tomorrow to another team and another until trade deadline. We really are happy for you to return. I'll have my assistant send you all the information on your return to LA."

"Alright, sir. Thank you."

Trying to absorb all this information, I still couldn't believe this was happening. I didn't want to go to LA or anywhere for that matter if Arianna wasn't with me.

My phone rang again, thinking it was another GM telling me I've been traded again. This time it said *Dad*.

"Hey, Dad."

"Blake, I heard you've been traded."

"How did you know? Did you have anything to do with the trade?"

"I convinced both general managers to make a deal. I've known them for a while and they owed me one."

"What the hell?!"

"Watch your tone. Son, you were born a Crusader and will leave your legacy with them as your grandfather and I did. There's no compromise."

Staying silent, I clenched my free hand tightly into a fist. My heart pounded so hard I thought it was going to explode out of my chest. Heat rushed up my neck and flushed my cheeks.

"I told you that Storm owner was trouble. Did you know that they're going bankrupt?"

"What the hell are you talking about, Dad?" My voice got louder.

"Elliott told me that they're looking for another owner since they're losing money. Plus, Elliott mentioned you and Arianna are spending too much time together. It looks bad on Arianna and your career."

"Dad, you always do this. You meddle in my career. This is *my* hockey career. I will go wherever I am led to. I don't need my father convincing another team to buy me back."

"Blake—" Dad's voice got louder and much sterner.

"Listen, Dad. I am not done talking. I need you to stop interfering with my career and now my relationships. If in fact, the Storm is going bankrupt, then Arianna can fix it. I know she can."

There was an awkward silence on the phone.

"I need to pack. I'm probably going to fly out to LA later today." Then I hung up the phone on my dad, not letting him get the last word anymore.

28

ARIANNA

After my panic attack, I excused myself to my room to lie down and rest. I didn't want to talk to anyone at this point. I needed to tell Blake that we couldn't see each other anymore, but I needed to tell him in person. Doing it over the phone or through text was not my style, although I'd never broken up with anyone before. I've had my heart broken many times... by the same guy.

I took an Ativan to help calm me down. When I had my first panic attack, I thought I was having a heart attack so Kuya Eric took me to the hospital, and they told me it was stress and anxiety. Since then, my doctor prescribed me an antidepressant and anti-anxiety medication. I didn't take it often because of the side effects. One of which was getting lethargic and sleepy. I changed into my pajamas, brushed my teeth, and took my contacts out. Heaviness weighed on my eyelids, I could barely keep them open. My brain was foggy and I yawned a few times. I laid down and drifted off to sleep.

My alarm clock woke me up from my long night of sleeping. I was groggy, still drowsy from the medication. My head continued to feel pretty foggy. Even though I slept for about twelve hours, it didn't seem like I slept at all. After a few minutes of sitting up in bed, I finally was alert enough to go use the bathroom and take a shower.

I took a long, hot shower this morning, and replayed everything that occurred yesterday. My body went stiff, and I put my hand over my mouth.

"Oh shit!" I completely forgot to FaceTime Blake last night. There was so much I was dealing with yesterday, that I knocked out after I took my anti-anxiety med.

I jumped out of the shower and got dressed quickly. Then I grabbed my cell phone from my side table in my bedroom. *Great!* My phone was not turning on. The battery died. I plugged it in to charge and turned on my phone. After a minute, my phone was up and running. I saw a few voicemails and texts from Blake. I texted him back.

Good morning, handsome. I'm so sorry about last night. My phone died, and I was so exhausted that I fell asleep early. I hope to video chat with you soon. I know you have a game tonight. Good luck! I miss you more than you know. Xo

I waited for fifteen minutes and there wasn't a text response from Blake. He was probably at morning skate. I wouldn't get too worried about it though. I hoped he'd call or text me before the game later. I listened to the voice mails that he left last night. You can hear the anguish in his voice. He was truly worried about me. I hoped that he was able to get some sleep knowing that I hadn't responded to let him know that I was safe.

I went downstairs and grabbed something to take with me on the road. I wanted to visit Lolo Tony this morning at the hospital and go to the office thereafter since I had an important meeting at ten a.m.

"Daddy!" I yelled out in the quiet home.

I searched for Daddy around the house, but noticed his car was missing in the garage. He had left the house already for the day. I got into my car and drove off to Sequoia Grove Hospital.

KNOCK. KNOCK. "LOLO TONY," I said softly as I walked inside his room. Jessa was sitting at his bedside and turned to face me when I quietly stepped through the door to relieve her for a bit. Lola Lynn was planning to relieve me in a couple hours so I could go to the office.

"Hey, Jessa. How's it going?" I gave her a kiss on the cheek and a hug, then pulled up a chair next to her.

"It's alright. Lolo's been sleeping for a while. I'm getting kind of worried."

"How long have you been here?"

"Since last night. How are things at the office? Kuya Eric texted that you had a panic attack last night."

"I'm fine now. I've been so stressed out. It seems that this business investment that Lolo gave me may not have been as good of an investment as he may have hoped."

"I know you, Ari, and you can overcome any challenge."

"Thanks, cousin." I smiled, feeling somewhat reassured.

"Are you good, Ari? I'm getting sleepy and want to get home to rest for a bit."

"I'll be fine. Drive safely." Jessa stood up and gave me a hug. Then we said our 'goodbyes.'

A few minutes later, I heard the rustling of the sheets. I watched Lolo Tony to make sure he was okay. He was convulsing and restless, which was out of character. I think he was having a seizure. I've never seen him like this since he was admitted to Sequoia Grove. His eyes were still closed. I reached for the call button and pressed the red button to alert the nurse to come into the room. Then I ran into the hallway.

"Nurse! My grandpa needs help!" I shouted impatiently.

"Hi, is everything okay?" the older Filipino woman wearing teal green scrubs asked as she quickly entered the room and saw Lolo Tony shaking.

She got closer to our grandfather, and he stopped suddenly, just lying there. "Mr. Santos." She touched his shoulder and tried to wake him. "Mr. Santos." She used her first two fingers and placed them on his inner wrist, probably checking his pulse, then the nurse pressed the blue button on the wall, which had a voice on the hospital loudspeaker announcing that there was a code blue in this room.

Abruptly getting up from my chair, I stepped back as a clinical team of nurses and doctors came running into the room. Someone rolled a crash cart inside the room, and someone else placed an oxygen mask over his nose and mouth and pumped air into him.

Oh my God! Tears fell down my cheeks as I watched the hospital staff try to save him. Did I just witness Lolo Tony dying? I gasped and covered my mouth with my hand, eyes opened wide, bewildered at what was going on. Was this really happening?

After a few minutes of trying to resuscitate my grandfather, one of the doctor's stopped and informed the team to do the same. He looked at the clock and declared time of death.

That same doctor stepped toward me until he was standing right in front of me. His eyes sympathetic. He placed his hand on my upper arm.

"I'm sorry. We couldn't save him."

I nearly fell over. Luckily, there was a wall I was able to lean against. I completely lost it. I was hyperventilating, gasping for air in between breaths and crying out loud. I couldn't slow down my breathing. I couldn't believe this. My rock... the patriarch of the Santos family... was gone.

29

ARIANNA

I called my receptionist and informed her that I would be taking a few days off from work to be with my family. I postponed the emergency board meeting, but this took precedence, and I knew that I wouldn't be able to focus. News broke out about Lolo Tony's death around Storm headquarters. I've been receiving tons of texts, calls, and emails from my staff with condolences, and 'please let me know if there is anything I can do for you and your family.' *Yes, if you can bring Lolo Tony back, please do it.*

My family had been congregating at Lolo Tony and Lola Lynn's house in the city every evening to do the rosary and say prayers both in English and Tagalog. I had spent a lot of my day at their home since Lolo's death. I've kept Lola Lynn company and helped her sort through all of Lolo's belongings, pictures for the collage and montage for his viewing, and an outfit for him to wear in the casket. There was so much preparation that went into planning a funeral. It's expected that a couple hundred people, specifically family, friends, and Lolo's old colleagues would be attending the viewing and funeral.

Lolo was a well-respected and honest man. He also served as

a special agent for the President of the Philippines before he met Lola Lynn and came to the States in the 1970s. He didn't have much but had the business smarts to grow the empire that Daddy runs to this day... SV Communications, a full-service digital public relations and marketing firm that services the top leading Silicon Valley technology, healthcare, and IT companies.

I admired Lolo Tony for all he had done for our family. He believed in me to run a hockey franchise, and I won't let him down. I will need to take a better look at the financials. As I sorted through all of Lolo's documents, I came across the contract for the change in ownership for the Storm organization, legal documents, and the financials of the franchise.

I skimmed through the financials and the numbers seemed different from the ones I received yesterday. I analyzed the numbers for hours yesterday afternoon. I'm sure the numbers were the same as my report. Putting it off to the side, I continued to go through the rest of his documents. Lolo Tony would want me to figure things out on my own if there were issues with the business. He trusted me with it and I will overcome the challenges I'm faced with.

It was Friday and Blake and the team had supposedly returned to San Francisco last night, but I didn't get a chance to talk to him yesterday, so I'm not sure if he was back or not. He never responded to my text from the other day, but I haven't followed up with him either. I've been so busy with Lolo Tony's funeral preparations.

Hi handsome. I haven't heard from you in a couple days. Are you back in the city? I've missed you! Please call me. I need to talk to you. Xo

I put my phone down and went back to helping Lola Lynn in her room. Lola took out some clothes from the closet.

"Ari, anak, how about this?" She was holding up a sheer cream-colored top with embroidery on it and black slacks. "The barong Tagalog was specially made for him for your parents' wedding."

"Lola, it's perfect. With a white undershirt, he will look good for heaven." I gave a small smile.

"Hopefully not good enough for him to find a girlfriend up there." My grandmother laughed. She had a big grin on her face.

"LOLA!" I laughed out loud. "You know you're his forever love. You've been together over fifty years." I got up and draped my arms around her shoulders from the side and squeezed.

"I know... your Lolo is my one and only love and will always be until we see each other again."

My heart just melted. Their relationship as well as my parents' were serious goals for me. I wanted to be with someone who respected my family and understood that family came first.

I received an incoming text message from an unknown number:

Hello Miss Santos,

My name is Katherine Mendoza and I'm an investigative reporter. I received some information about your franchise that I think you should know about. Can we meet?

Interesting. I didn't know how this person got my phone number, but I was definitely curious about the information she had about my organization. I did a quick internet search and found some highly regarded articles she wrote that won her several awards.

I texted Katherine back and told her where to meet me in an hour.

ARRIVING EARLY at the Starbucks in Union Square next door to the Sir Francis Drake Hotel, I found a table in the corner in the back of the room where it seemed to have more privacy as I waited for Katherine to arrive. I chose this place, so I could surprise Blake after my meeting since we've been missing each other on the phone. Scrolling through my phone, I received a text message from Kuya Eric:

Hey Ari, did you hear? Blake got traded back to LA last night. I saw these and thought you may want to see this.

My brother sent me a few pictures of what looks like other hockey players at a club. One of the pictures was of Blake with a couple beautiful women. He looked way too happy and too comfy with the ladies.

I clenched my jaw. My blood boiled and I wanted to fucking scream. *What the hell?!* Blake was traded back to LA and looked like he was celebrating with his teammates.

Hey Blake, when were you going to tell me that you were traded and moved back to LA? It looked like you forgot about me pretty quickly and were happy to be back to your old habits. Don't bother calling me.

I sent Blake the picture Kuya Eric sent me, then put my phone away as I saw a pretty brunette walk toward me. I took a couple deep breaths in and out to prepare myself for this meeting.

"Miss Santos, nice to meet you." She shook my hand before sitting down. "I wanted to give you my deepest condolences on the loss of your grandfather. I actually had the pleasure of meeting him when he obtained ownership of the franchise."

"Miss Mendoza, nice to meet you as well. And thank you. I appreciate the condolences."

Katherine spoke softly, "When I met Mr. Santos, he mentioned that he was giving the business to you. He read some of my investigative news articles on some businesses that I found were doing shady business, so he asked me to look into the Storm franchise."

"I see. What did Lolo Tony think was happening?"

"He believed that the financials were not reported correctly. He was right." Katherine took out some papers from her bag and handed them to me. "This is the article that I would like to report."

It took me a couple minutes to read. My eyes widened. This was the information I needed to prove the financials were off.

"Miss Mendoza, I assume you have proof of the statements you made in the article?"

"Yes, right here." Katherine took more papers out of her bag and handed them to me.

"Perfect. May I keep these please?"

"Of course, those are your copies."

"I wanted to ask you something. You mentioned earlier that Lolo Tony had a feeling that someone was doing some shady business in my organization. Who gave you the information you needed to prove that this person was doing illegal business transactions?"

"It was a whistleblower at the company. One of the assistants in the finance department. But I received a call from one of your players yesterday, concerned that the Storm franchise was going bankrupt and was asking for my help."

"Who was that?"

"Blake Collins."

"Oh. Well, Miss Mendoza, thank you for reaching out to me. I appreciate all the information."

"Good luck, Miss Santos."

Katherine got up, shook my hand, and walked out of the coffee shop.

The franchise messed with the wrong family.

30

BLAKE

Tomorrow was the day of Antonio Santos, Sr.'s funeral. As someone who has met him and known him for a short time, he asked me to promise him to take care of Arianna and help her with the Storm franchise. I couldn't do that now. Arianna broke up with me and told me our relationship was strictly professional.

I wanted to attend the funeral and pay my respects to Tony and his family. I had a plane ticket ready for my short trip to San Francisco, but I was having second thoughts. I didn't want to be in the same room with Arianna. For the first time in my life, I fell in love with someone, a woman who pushed me out of my comfort zone and challenged me. I loved Arianna, but she didn't want me anymore. I called, left voice messages, and texted her with no response back. She sent me a picture of me partying with women, but that picture was not even recent. I wanted her to hear it from me personally to explain everything.

If I attended the funeral, I'm not sure how I would feel seeing Arianna again. As I contemplated what I needed to do, I turned on the television at my home in Los Angeles. I called and spoke with Maggie yesterday on my way to LA to let her know to put my listing on hold since my plans changed, and I ended up back here. Maggie told me that someone had made an offer already and it was still processing, but it was okay to stay at my house in the meantime until escrow closes.

I flipped the channel to ESPN and surprised to see Arianna's beautiful face on television. The reporters were talking about the Storm organization. Video footage of Elliott, along with some executives from the organization, including the Chief Financial Officer, was displayed on the screen. They all were handcuffed and escorted out of Storm headquarters by several police officers and the FBI. *Whatever they did must be a serious crime to have the FBI there.*

Arianna was being interviewed by the press. "I cannot go into detail at this time as they all are being charged with something, but I can assure you all that the San Francisco Storm will not have to endure dishonest conduct within the organization any longer." Arianna's facial expression was serious; however, her eyes were dull. There was no sparkle or life in them. She looked worn out.

The reporter asked Arianna questions regarding the structure of the organization, and Arianna's responded, "I will be doing major restructuring of the organization. We will make the announcements as soon as we've confirmed who will be taking on the roles for the positions in the organization."

AFTER ARIANNA'S interview on television, I texted her.

Hey Ari, I saw you on the news. I'm sorry that you had to deal with the mess of the organization. I'm also sorry that I didn't tell you I was traded, but please believe me when I tell you that picture you sent is not even close to being recent. I

don't know where you found that, but that was from about three years ago. Please call me. I need you.

I packed my stuff and started my eight-hour trip back to the San Francisco Bay Area. If Arianna didn't want to talk to me on the phone, I was going to her. She needed me as much as I needed her. I contacted Sam Cunningham on the way home and told him that I had an emergency that needed my attention and that I was thinking of doing an early retirement. *I will no longer be part of the Crusaders.*

Sam told me, "Blake, I understand. We wish you all the best."

I was going through a list of things I needed to do before I arrived in San Francisco. I still needed to figure out how I was going to approach Arianna. I wanted to surprise her, not tell her that I was coming home until I got there.

I called Maggie again and left her a voice message.

"Hey, Maggie. Blake Collins here. I am heading back to the Bay Area. Let me know when my house officially closes and I will hire movers to pack and move all my stuff. Call me if you have any questions. Thanks."

I called my dad. I thought it would be best for me to tell him that I left the Crusaders and I 'retired' early.

"Hey, Dad."

"Hey, Blake. Everything alright?" Dad's voice was different. Much calmer... but it wouldn't be for long.

"Yes, it is. I wanted to tell you something. It's not easy to say this, but I am retiring early. I told Sam Cunningham that I cannot be with the Crusaders anymore."

There was a long pause and an awkward silence.

"Dad? You still there?"

"Yes," he said in a low voice. "I saw the news about the Storm organization and the interview with Arianna. You're going back to San Francisco for her, aren't you?"

"She needs my help. You wouldn't understand and you don't

care. Dad, I love her, and I want to take care of her. I promised her grandfather I would."

"That's where you're wrong, son. I do care and have always wanted the best for you. That's why I'm so hard on you with hockey. You deserve the best."

That was the first time my dad actually opened up to me. "Umm... thanks?" I was caught off guard but tried to maintain my composure and keep my eye on the road.

"I'm being serious, Blake. I'm working on being a better father to you and Melissa. I spoke with your mom, and she's talked some sense into me for a change."

I laughed. "Mom's very smart."

"Yeah, she is. She married me, didn't she?" He laughed out loud, which made me laugh.

"Well, Blake, I hope things work out with Arianna, and we get to meet her soon."

"Thanks, Dad, for the talk. We'll talk again soon."

"Bye, son." I hung up the phone in the car.

Wow. So that's what it's like to have a decent conversation with my dad. Not bad.

I made reservations at the Sir Francis Drake Hotel. I was happy that they had vacancies. When I arrived in San Francisco, it was already late evening. Arianna hadn't called or texted me back. I decided that it would be best to just see Arianna tomorrow when I attended her grandfather's funeral. I wanted to show Arianna that I did care about her and her family. She was the most important person to me.

THE MORNING of Tony's funeral, I dressed in the darkest suit I had. I texted a couple of the Storm players and asked if they had the information for the funeral this morning. Brandon was the first to text me with the location and time for the service. I headed to the church for mass and blended in with the guys on the team. I don't think Arianna saw me. She was crying so much and had her oversized dark sunglasses on the entire time. There were a couple hundred people there. The church pews were filled. Hearing the eulogy about Tony's life, I wished I was able to meet him and get to know him before. He seemed like an amazing person.

After the mass, we were on the way to the cemetery for the burial. It was a very somber day in the city. It was overcast, but as soon as we were at the cemetery, the sun peeked out from the clouds as if it knew that we were celebrating Tony's life and that he was being welcomed into heaven.

We stood around the plot, listening to the priest give his sermon before they lowered the casket. Grabbing a rose from the funeral wreath, we all waited to throw it into the grave. We had an opportunity to pass by family and give them our condolences. That was my opportunity to let Arianna know I was there for her.

It was my turn to throw my rose into Tony's grave. I gave a silent prayer and threw my rose in. En route to where I was standing with the team, I stopped by the Santos family and shook hands, and offered them my condolences. When I got to Arianna, she stood up, removed her sunglasses, and was astonished to see me. Her eyes were red and puffy from crying so much and her cheeks were red.

"Blake, you're here. I thought you would be in LA since I haven't returned your calls or texts," she said softly and looked down.

I pushed her chin up, so I could look into her eyes. "I wanted to be here for you, Arianna. I don't want to be anywhere else if you're not with me."

She smiled and wrapped her arms around my waist. "I'm so sorry for everything, Blake."

I draped my arms around her shoulders, and she laid her

head on my chest. *I missed this. I missed her.* "No need to be sorry. I'm here. I also wanted to pay my respects to your Lolo Tony and make sure you were okay."

"Look at you saying Filipino words." She smiled. "I appreciate it so much that you're here. Would you mind sitting next to me?"

"Only if it's okay with your family."

Arianna turned her head to look at her family, and they all welcomed me with open arms to sit with them. "My family is more than happy to have you sit with us."

I gave a small smile to everyone and softly said 'thank you.' I sat next to Arianna and held her hand, reassuring her that I was there for her, always.

Two Months Later

I received a call from Sloan that the sale on my condo finally closed. I am officially a homeowner in beautiful San Francisco. Sloan's assistant dropped off the house keys to me, and I scheduled movers to bring my belongings to my new home. I was so excited, but wanted to keep this as a surprise for Arianna.

Hi, beautiful. I have a surprise to show you later this evening. I'll come up to your office when you're ready. Xo

Arianna replied back.

Hey, handsome. You know I hate surprises! But sure, I'll let you know when I'm done for the day. I can't wait to see you, my love. Xo

Arianna and I had a long talk about what happened with Elliott and the rest of the executives that were arrested. I couldn't believe that asshole thought he could outsmart the Santos family. Those so-called executives have been embezzling the Storm organization's finances for years and changing up the financial legends so it would seem the organization was gaining a profit. Elliott suggested that Arianna schedule an emergency meeting to discuss financials, but his plan was to tell Arianna that the company was bankrupt and convince her to sell it. Elliott was going to buy the franchise. That was his plan the entire time.

Arianna mentioned that the day Elliott got arrested, she asked him why. His response was 'because *you* are the owner. I befriended Tony when he purchased the franchise. He told me his plan was to give all this to you. I wanted to purchase the franchise. I've lived and breathed hockey since I was young. I placed a bid to buy this organization, but I lost to *your* family, who knows *nothing* about hockey.' With the help of an investigative reporter, Katherine Mendoza, Arianna filed charges against all the perpetrators and hopefully will get the money they stole returned back to the franchise.

A few hours later, I picked up Arianna at her office.

"Hey, beautiful." I went through the office doorway.

"I don't get tired of hearing that from you." She smiled at me.

"Good. Because I won't ever stop calling you that." I winked at her. "Are you ready?"

"For you handsome... always." Arianna winked back.

Arianna grabbed her belongings. I took them from her, so she didn't have to lift a finger. I held her hand instead and we went down to the elevator. We didn't need to hide our relationship anymore... now that she appointed me as the new general manager of the Storm.

When we got inside my car, I put a blindfold on her.

"Is this really necessary, Blake?"

"Yes, Arianna." I waved my hand in front of her face to see if she could see what I was doing, but she didn't say anything.

"How many fingers am I holding up?" I wasn't holding up my hand or my fingers.

"I don't know, two?"

"Okay, you can't see. Perfect."

"Blakey, hurry up, get to our destination. I don't like being this vulnerable. It's freaking me out."

"Yes, Ari. I'm going."

After fifteen minutes of driving around San Francisco and getting weird looks from other drivers who pulled next to my car seeing Arianna blindfolded, we made it to the new condo. I opened the passenger door and led Arianna safely to the property. I unlocked the front door, took Arianna's hand, and led her over the threshold.

"Are you ready, beautiful?"

"Yes, I'm ready."

I removed the blindfold. Arianna looked around the foyer of the condo. She was smiling, her dark brown eyes gleamed with excitement.

"I'm an official homeowner and San Francisco resident."

Arianna turned to face me and gave me a long, passionate kiss.

"I'm so happy for you, Blakey."

"Well, I still need to get my things moved here from storage, but I have some belongings here already."

"It will feel like home," Arianna said.

"Ari, it won't feel like home unless you're here with me. I want this condo to be your home too."

"Are you serious?"

"Yes, so what do—"

She interrupted me with another passionate kiss, her tongue explored the depths of my mouth. When we came up for air, I tried to catch my breath.

"So that means you'll stay here with me?" I said in a low, breathy voice.

"Of course!" Arianna smiled wide from ear to ear. "How about we make this agreement official?"

"What do you have in mind?" I raised an eyebrow, curious to hear what she was going to say.

Arianna took my hand. "Take me to *our* bedroom. Do you have your jersey here?" She smirked and winked at me.

I knew what she wanted to do, and I'm sure we would be celebrating like that more often now that we'd be living together.

EPILOGUE

ARIANNA

The San Francisco Storm made it to the Stanley Cup Finals against our rivals, the California Crusaders. It's the battle of Northern and Southern California. We were up three games to one, and now playing at home. We needed to win this game to clinch the series and finally be champions. I have faced many challenges and adversity as the owner of the team, and I needed this win to prove that I can indeed handle this job title.

Since Blake's return to San Francisco and back to me, he

had been nothing but supportive in all the decisions we made for the Storm. Blake and I watched all the home games from the presidential suite of the SV Communications Arena in San Francisco. My entire family as well as my best friends were here with me tonight, which was odd because it was usually only one or two that would attend a game with me. Blake's family flew in from Canada to witness tonight's game as well. This was the second time they met my family and friends, and they seemed to get along well. This was an important game for our families, I'm guessing that's probably why they were all here. I wished Lolo Tony and Mama were here to see history be made in the National Hockey League. I had Mama's locket on and touched it. It carried both Mama and Lolo's pictures in it.

I looked around at everyone in the suite. There was lots of laughter, drinking, and well-dressed people here. Daddy once told me that since I was the owner, I needed to dress nicely for the games since there will always be some type of media coverage, and 'we always needed to look presentable.' You never knew how the media would react to what they saw on camera. That was a lesson I learned recently. Plus, if we won game five, we would win the Stanley Cup, and there would definitely be tons of media coverage of me, Blake, our families, and the team. I wore a form-fitting black dress, black patent leather Louboutin booties, and a navy blue blazer.

Watching Blake become the general manager of the Storm, made my heart melt. He was truly happy in his new role and helped his team succeed in a different way. Plus, he looked fine as hell wearing his tailored suits. He looked extra sexy and scrumptious for tonight's game. As we sat there watching our team on the ice while holding hands, I leaned in close to his ear.

"Blakey, you are looking extra sexy and delectable tonight. I really hope the Storm win. I know one way we can celebrate if they do," I whispered and watched Blake squirm in his seat. His slacks were a skinny fit and a slight bulge was growing in the front.

"Look what you do to me... can you get me your purse, Ari?"

I gave him my purse and he put it on his lap to cover his hard length protruding from his dress pants.

I gazed at him and laughed. Leaning toward his ear again, I whispered, "Just think of your dad."

Blake looked back at his dad, who was conversing with my uncle and dad. "Thanks, that helped. Don't do that again," he whispered and had a large grin on his face.

I winked at him, then gave him a sweet kiss on his cheek.

"I love you."

"I love you too, beautiful."

First period was nearly over with one goal scored by the Storm and the Crusaders were scoreless.

Blake turned to me. "It's almost intermission. You know who's performing, right?"

"Of course, I do! It's Maroon 5! My favorite band! I was so stoked when I found out they were performing tonight." I shrieked like a total fangirl.

"Well, guess what? We're going to be the ones introducing them to the crowd so you're going to see them up close. Plus, the whole family can come down to watch the performance as well."

"Oh my God, Blake! That sounds so amazing!" I looked over at center ice and could see the band setting up. "I'm so excited! Are we going to go down there now?"

"Yes, beautiful. Soak in this moment, okay?"

"Of course, I will, handsome."

A few minutes later, Blake and I, as well as our families, were downstairs on the lower level by the glass. The band looked like they were almost ready to play. There was a red carpet rolled out toward center ice by the Storm logo on the floor. I squeezed Blake's hand in excitement but remained as composed as I could be. The lights turned off. Blake pulled my arm, and we started walking to the open door where the red carpet began.

The lights slowly brightened up the ice rink to a low light setting, focusing only on center ice. A spotlight was focused on Blake and me at the beginning of the red carpet aisle. Blake turned to me and smiled.

"Ready?"

I smiled. "Yes."

Still hand in hand, we slowly walk down the red carpet. I looked to see both the San Francisco Storm and California Crusaders on either side of the carpet. The players held their hockey sticks up high, forming an arch. *This is fancy!* I was impressed. We finally reached center ice and the end of the red carpet where Maroon 5 was getting ready to perform. One of the arena staff handed Blake a microphone. Blake let go of my hand and faced me. He reached inside his coat and took something out. Then he knelt down on one knee.

Oh my God! Is this what I think it is? My heartbeat raced and flutters were felt in my stomach.

Blake placed the little red box on the carpet. He held the microphone in one hand and held my hand in the other, quivering. "Arianna, you are the most gorgeous woman in the entire world. Your beauty not only radiates on the outside, but on the inside as well. You are the most selfless, thoughtful, and caring person I have ever known, you put others' needs first before your own."

Tears started falling down my cheeks. I was in shock and so happy. I stared into Blake's hazel-green eyes and saw he had a tear falling from the corner of his eye. *I hoped I wouldn't pass out.*

"You are strong and will fight for what's right. You are amazing. Every day is a new and exciting journey with you, and I would be honored to be the man that can spend his entire life with you. Arianna Santos, will you do me the honor of being my wife?"

Blake placed the microphone down and picked up the small red Cartier box and opened it up, flashing a large cushion cut diamond with two diamond baguettes on either side of the center stone and small diamonds around the band.

I placed my hands over my mouth, not believing that this was really happening to me. "Yes!" I nodded my head and said it with a trembling voice simultaneously.

Blake got up quickly and wrapped his arms around me, kissing me with so much passion. He placed the ring on my left hand. Maroon 5 started performing "Sugar." Our families and friends rushed onto the ice to be with us. The players of both teams congratulated us. The crowd was going wild.

I admired the ring, with tears still flowing down my face. I probably looked like a hot mess, but I didn't care. I'm engaged to the man of my dreams.

"I love you, handsome. Well played."

"I love you too, beautiful...I've always been playing for you."

THE END

ALSO BY AURORA PAIGE

Hot On Ice Series

Playing for You (Hot on Ice, Book 1) -
https://www.amazon.com/dp/B08NHVQTKY

Playing for Keeps (Hot on Ice, Book 2) -
https://www.amazon.com/dp/B09L891G3P/

Playing for Us (Hot on Ice, Book 3) -
https://www.amazon.com/dp/B0B54JF4LW/

Hot for the Holidays Series

Merry In Mykonos - https://www.amazon.com/dp/B08P3QVYMG

Unmasked: A Fairytale Retelling -
https://www.amazon.com/dp/B08R9B1QZJ

Curves for Christmas Series

All Wrapped Up (Book 10) - https://www.amazon.com/dp/B0982J63FK

Man of the Month Club - Starlight Bay Series

Jingle on the Bay (December) -
https://www.amazon.com/dp/B08X1C95LN

The Holidates Series

The Christmas Rental (Book 1) -
https://www.amazon.com/dp/B09G15P7MG

The Love Prescription (Book 2) -
https://www.amazon.com/dp/B09GNWFHSX

Moonstruck at Mardi Gras (Book 16) -
https://www.amazon.com/dp/B0B54JMQ7M

Daddy's Little Princess (Book 24) by Aurora Paige & Josie O'Sullivan - https://www.amazon.com/dp/B0BQ1L9F2G *(Coming Soon)*

Midnight Kisses Series

Secret Kisses - https://www.amazon.com/dp/B09G14XB2R

ABOUT AURORA PAIGE

Aurora Paige is a Filipina-American writer of steamy contemporary multicultural romance with sassy heroines and sexy heroes. Her books deliver a variety of curvy heroines, alpha heroes, multicultural and interracial relationships, steamy heat, and a guaranteed happily ever after.

Be sure to sign up for my newsletter http://www.aurorapaige. com/newsletter-sign-up to stay updated on new releases, exclusive content, events, and freebies! If you loved this story and wanted to connect with other readers of my books, join us in my Facebook group: http://www.facebook.com/groups/ thesmittensquad/

- f facebook.com/authoraurorapaige
- 𝕏 twitter.com/xoaurorapaige
- ⊙ instagram.com/xoaurorapaige
- g goodreads.com/aurorapaige
- a amazon.com/~/e/B08M91XPXB
- ⓟ pinterest.com/xoaurorapaige
- BB bookbub.com/authors/aurora-paige
- ♪ tiktok.com/@xoaurorapaige

ACKNOWLEDGMENTS

When I went to my first NHL hockey game to watch the San Jose Sharks play the Los Angeles Kings many years ago, I instantly fell in love with the sport. That's when I knew that I wanted my first full-length novel and series to be a sports romance.

It took me some time to get this book out in the world, but I finally did it! *insert happy tears*

And now for my thank you speech...

First and foremost, **I'd like to thank the love of my life, S.** - Thank you babe for holding down the fort and giving me the time to write in the wee hours of the night. You don't know how much it means to me. As Tony Stark would say, 'I love you, 3000!'

To my son, B., and fur daughter, B. - Thank you for bringing so much joy in my life, especially during the days where I'm worn out and exhausted. I love you both to infinity and beyond!

To my family and friends - I appreciate all the love and support you have provided to me. Thank you for putting up with me when I had to reschedule and cancel plans so I could meet deadlines.

To my PA, Ashley Blank - Thank you so much for all you've done to help me build my brand and sharing my vision to the world. I'm forever grateful that our paths crossed! Love you boo!

Alessandra Torre - Thank you for all your assistance and support through your bootcamp to get this book started and done! Thank you for introducing me to **Ellie (My Brother's Editor)**!

Ellie - Thank you for dealing with a newb like me and getting this bad boy ready to publish!

Thank you to all those that took a chance on me and read my book baby. It means so much to me! *more happy tears* Thank you for your support with your reviews, beautiful edits, and sharing my book through bookstagram and social media. Words cannot express how grateful I am for all your support. My heart if overflowing with gratitude. xoxo

A NOTE FROM AURORA

Before you go, may I ask you for a quick favor?

Yay! I knew I could count on you.

Would you please leave this book a review on Amazon? Reviews are very important for authors, as they help us sell more books. This will in turn enable me to write more books for you.

Please take a quick minute to go to Amazon and leave this book an honest review. I promise it doesn't take very long, but it can help this book reach more readers just like you.

Thank you so much for reading, and thank you so much for being part of the journey.

XO,

Aurora Paige